STEVEN PAUL WATSON

FULL WOLF MOON

HOWLING MOON BOOK TWO

Full Wolf Moon

Howling Moon Book Two

This book is a work of fiction. The characters, incidents, and dialogue are drawn from the author's imagination and are not to be construed as real. Any resemblance to actual events or persons, living or dead, is entirely coincidental.

Published by Steven Paul Watson

ISBN-13: 979-8-218-07049-6

Visit the author at: www.stevenpaulwatson.com

Also available in ebook

With many special thanks to...

My, loving wife, Samantha, and her constant encouragement.

The many beta readers who have been along for the ride. And I want to thank those who read book one and kept asking me for book two. You all gave me the support and confidence to push through my own self-doubt when I needed it.

To Getcovers who took my vision of the cover and turned it in to something beyond my dreams. Immygrace who did a wonderful edit in cleaning up the stuff that I couldn't bring myself to change.

For

Sadie

Works by Steven Paul Watson

Howling Moon Series:

Howling Moon: The Beginning

Full Wolf Moon

Other Works:

Human 76 (Anthology Entry "The Hunted")

Chapter One

Emily Meyer splashed water on her face just as a fury of knocks clashed against the old metal door. The commotion echoed throughout the cramped gas station bathroom. "Come on!" a woman harshly called out from the other side of the rusted barrier. Emily heard the breathing of the angry woman so obviously tired of waiting. Emily was unsure of how long she'd been out there. It was deafening. The sound of each huff may have well derived from a category five hurricane to her ears.

Emily gasped the moment the pounding erupted again. "Give me a couple more minutes," she pleaded.

She might as well have been talking to the unrecognizable woman looking back at her from the dirty mirror. She tried to gather her emotions as she glared at the reflection, it may have only been a few months since the attack, but it looked and felt like years. Emily again took a deep breath, trying to gain some confidence as she grabbed the scissors and chopped at her tangled hair. It was an unimaginable mess and had gone too long without anything resembling proper care for her naturally curly hair. Even the bright red that she had been known for growing up now seemed a dim orange from lack of attention.

"Bitch." She heard the mumbled expletive from the other side of the door. The woman had barely said it as a whisper, but with Emily's enhanced hearing, she might as well have been yelling into a bullhorn. Emily smiled. So much about the new life she hated, but the enhanced senses were not one of them. It only took a couple of minutes to cut her way through her hair, and it looked worse now than before. As a deep-seated pang of regret ran through her, she bit down on her lower lip. She needed a shower and a good shampoo. *Or even a hot bath*, she thought, *a long hot bath would cure everything.*

Three jarring knocks came, louder and more forceful than before, making it feel as if the force of the knocks sent waves through the room. The smell of oil and sweat drifted into the room, causing panic in the pit of Emily's stomach as the crashes on the metal surface echoed in the tiny room. "Hurry up!" a male bellowed. There were no pleasantries in his tone, only anger.

Emily swiftly pushed all the loose hair from her shoulders into the sink. As much as she dreaded it, she would have to find a stream somewhere and bathe when she got an opportunity. She promptly pulled the large sweatshirt back over her head and tucked her freshly mangled curls back into the shadow of the large hood. Despite her overpowering scent, it still had Colin's aroma embedded in it. Each time she caught his scent, it simultaneously caused her to smile and broke her heart. Emily grabbed the ragged duffel bag at her feet before sliding the lock on the door with a slow shriek of metal on metal. It came open instantly from the other side. The man leaned against the edge, barely enough room for her to squeeze past. He smelled. His clothing matched his scent. He was covered in dirt and oil—an obvious mechanic trademark—and the smell of grease filled her nostrils, dulling all her other senses. She still didn't have complete control. It was always one or the other; she had yet to be able to push one sense to the side for another.

The girl smelled different. She stepped into Emily's path as she tried to navigate past the brute. She could smell his sweat on her skin and in her hair, but there was a sweet lavender scent as well.

"God, you reek." She held her hand over her mouth and nose. The two of them never made eye contact. She pinched her eyes closed to make it known that the smell was going as far as to affect her sight. Emily wondered if the woman noticed how her boyfriend smelled or if she just wanted to be rude to her. Emily lowered her head, keeping her eyes from making contact. She heard the girl speak again, the same small whisper. "Trash. What's the world coming to?"

Emily quickly grabbed a couple of bottles of water and a few snacks before rushing to the counter. She had been in there longer than she thought. The sun was starting to set. She rushed to get past a couple of men as they approached the register. She watched the cashier ring her stuff up, trying to ignore the heavy breathing and muffled laugh of the two men who had settled in behind her. She could see their reflection in the window, they were in football jerseys, barely old enough to buy the beer in their arms, and they ogled her with fierce determination as they were trying to memorize every unseen part of her body. She knew how she looked. The thought they might be into her still made her feel uneasy. She pulled the back of the sweatshirt down on her jeans. "Don't do that, baby. You've got a fine ass," one of the men said.

"Makes up for the crack whore smell," the other said, laughing. She could see the two of them bump fists to celebrate his vulgarity. "Bet if I had a pill bottle and shook it, you'd come running." Emily gritted her teeth; she was beginning to sweat. It was too hot to be in the large, hooded sweatshirt, and she pushed it off her face before she exchanged looks from the cashier to the reflection in the window. She saw the disgusted look on the cashier's face as she took her money, careful not to let their skin make contact. It wasn't directed at the two men either. Emily focused, seeing her distorted reflection in the glass. It looked so different from her tangled shoulder-length hair. The cashier returned the money, careful not to touch her still. The young woman sneered, not even trying in her swift motion dropping the money into Emily's palm. Emily's anger grew. She felt the wolf deep down in her stomach. It was dark now, it was sudden, and the wolf had more control when the sun was down. It didn't matter what cycle the moon was in; the wolf always wanted out when it was dark.

His hands were cold on her waist. "I bet you clean up real nice." She felt the first man's hot breath on the back of her neck. She pushed forcefully off the counter, turning, landing on top of him with enlarged canines, just missing the softness of his exposed neck as her jaws snapped fiercely. Emily felt the wolf's anger. It matched her own at the unwelcome touch of a stranger. The look he gave her was like he was doing her a favor by touching her. She could smell the blood pulsating through his veins, and she wanted to rip his throat open.

"What the fuck?" the other man questioned, quickly moving away, falling over a display of chips, scattering debris all around the store in a loud exchange of events.

Emily could smell the man under her. He had soiled himself. She smiled, wanting to laugh, but all that came was a huff of breath as she snarled. She felt her lip quiver under the presence of her extended canines. Her heart raced. She was enjoying the fear she put into the men who thought they were so much better than her.

"John… her teeth…." The couple from the bathroom was on the other side of her, having rushed to check out the commotion. She could smell their fear and hear their hearts race. The guy even stopped breathing at the sight of her. The brute of a man who was so threatening to her a moment earlier was a heartbeat from running, and she wanted him to. The wolf wanted him to as well so she could chase him down. But she couldn't let that happen no matter how badly she wanted to hurt the man. She knew if she let the wolf out here and now, she would be the only person to leave the gas station alive.

Emily jumped to her feet, pulling the hood back over her head as she hurried to the register. The cashier was nowhere to be seen. She grabbed her things from the counter before rushing out the door. "Damn it," she muttered. She rushed past the vehicles out from across the road, not looking in either direction or into the wilderness. She ran as fast as she could, heart racing with each padding of her worn-out shoes on wet ground. The wolf wanted to run. She could feel her heart racing and the growing ache in her stomach to let it out. With each quick step she took, she wanted to go faster. The wolf wanted to go faster. She stumbled, stepping on a dead log before tumbling to the ground. She screamed a shrill sound trying to get her anger and sorrow out of her body. This was her life now. Her few possessions spilled from the duffel bag, scattered with the unhealthy snack and water on the ground around her. She rested back on her knees, staring up at the moon, and attempted to scream again. At least that made her feel something. But what she released with her anger was a howl, wildlife around her running in terror as her voice deepened. She leaned forward. "No," she growled, looking at her long fingernails and disjointed knuckles. She would not let it out. She took long deep breaths; the shaking stopped upon standing. Quick to gather all her things before walking away at a calmer, more controlled pace.

It was easy to find the abandoned church. She crossed past her truck, carefully parked out of sight behind the crumbling structure. It was pitch-black now, but she had no problem seeing where she was going. Across the small porch, cautiously stepping on the solid planks remaining. It was obvious this was a party spot. She was watchful not to step on any of the garbage littering the porch, a mixture of broken bottles, fast-food wrappers, and even needles. She walked through the entrance. The doors themselves were long gone. Most of the pews were damaged, hit by baseball bats, she thought, leaving only splintered remains.

"Hello?"

She said it out of habit, hearing something scrambled away unseen. She knew there was no one there. She would have been able to smell if there was. The only scent remaining in the old church was her own.

Emily screamed. It was all she wanted, a break from her growing hunger. The wrenching pain caused her to double over on the ground. There had to be a way to make it stop. The pain made her see double when she could even see at all. She glanced around the lush forest floor and could barely make anything out. She knew she was being watched, but couldn't see her voyeur.

"Hello?" she spoke up through a gravelly voice, much more the other's tone than her own.

She held a tight grip on the shirt in hand. She dropped it to the bag when she felt the chill of a cold sweat run up her back.

"Hello?" she muttered, looking down at her shirt, debating whether she should put it back on. She felt the cool wind shift around her, taking a long deep breath, but no scents were lingering in the air. None human, anyways. She shifted her arms around to unclasp the black bra, and again, she felt the same intense feeling. Quickly, she turned. She knew her eyes had changed as her adrenaline began to pump, and everything in the forest changed color to dim grays and blacks.

Caw.

Caw.

Caw.

The crows sat on an old deadfall watching her, each of their eyes burrowing through her wanting to witness the horror of her transformation. Even then, she knew it was not the cause of the discomfort of knowing she was being watched. There was someone else or something there staring her down. It would be dark soon, and she was wasting time.

"I don't want to hurt you."

She watched the nearest crow as it observed her with eager curiosity. She could see her reflection in its dark amber eyes, and a smirk graced her lips. She gasped for air, but nothing seemed to catch as she stepped backward, falling to the ground. It was far too late now to stop the transformation.

"The Cherokee believed the crow to be a sign of transformation, not the carrion of death or bad omen most view them nowadays." Emily quickly turned back to the way she looked before, and it felt as if she'd been hit in the stomach. "Norse Pagans believed they carried messages from the dead…some messages from even Odin himself if you believe it."

"Lauren…" Her voice was more animal now than she could ever remember.

"In the flesh, of sorts." The woman smiled, picking the red shirt up off the bags, exposing the chains still stashed inside. "I remember those days."

"I'm dreaming…"

"You should know this by now, sweets." Lauren smiled. "We're all here." She tapped her finger on Emily's temple. "Right here in your head, waiting for others to come to join."

Emily looked up into the woman's intense eyes, more animal than her own. "Why are you here? Why now?"

"Because you're better than this," Lauren said, motioning toward the bag at her feet. "Loneliness and trying to fight who you are, what you have become… is the same thing that happened to me until the night I crossed paths with a serial killer. I know better than anyone that the emptiness inside is hard to fill, and if you spend too much time hiding from the rest of the world, you will become me. You will fall into the arms of someone who will embrace the other part of you. The wolf is a hunter, a killer by nature, not you, Emily. You must learn to control the wolf and embrace it as being part of you without becoming me, without becoming a predator."

Chapter Two

Emily moved from street to street, the jacket pulled tightly around her body. Oakridge was a small community hidden in the Umpqua National Forest of Oregon. If someone had looked, they wouldn't have even been able to find it on a map. She was surprised. She'd grown up in Williamson, West Virginia, and it was small, but it was not isolated—not like this. Twenty miles or more between towns and hardly any houses or off roads between them, this was isolation. So much wilderness she could hide here. Maybe even let the wolf run. The idea of letting the other part of her out brought a smile to her face. Despite everything that had happened, the reality, Lauren was right in her dream. She needed a way to let the wolf out to keep her humanity.

Rosie's was on the corner of the street. She could smell the fresh food from the walls, forcing her stomach to growl. She had so little money, and she knew how she looked. She ducked into the alley behind the mom-and-pop diner, quickly moving through the narrow street between the diner and a shutdown lawyer's office. She tossed the lid of the dumpster open with such fierce intention it caused her to look back at the back door of the diner in hopes it didn't draw anyone out. The smell made her stomach churn in disgust, followed by the hunger, having picked up the smell of something fresh from the filth inside. Or maybe she was just so hungry that it didn't matter anymore.

"Meara, quit feeding those damn strays!" she heard the harsh male voice yell out just as the back door of Rosie's opened. Emily saw the young woman with her blonde hair step out just before she dropped out of sight behind the rusted structure.

"Bite me. I heard them out here, and I'm going to feed them!" the young woman shouted back. Emily could hear the laughter in the young woman's voice. She could hear the grumbling coming from the inside as a response to her childish retort.

It was only a moment before the cats appeared, one, then two, up to six of them scrambling past Emily to the door. The seventh and final, a young calico, stopped and meowed when their eyes met. Emily could see the hairs on the cat's mane stand at attention. And then the loud hiss, so vigorous it was hard to imagine it escaping such a small body as it bounced several steps backward from Emily.

"Are you hungry?" the young woman questioned.

Emily held her breath, careful not to move. The small cat's eyes were still glued to her as it circled away from her, its fear not enough to stop it from pursuing a free meal. Emily knew the feeling.

"I thought I saw someone… the cat confirms it…" She heard the young woman step out into the open. She imagined thick-soled combat boots on the wet concrete.

Emily pulled the hood tightly over her head, twisting, looking for a way to escape without being seen. There were none.

"Just stay there." She could hear the woman backtrack. Emily stood hearing the door to the diner shut, only a couple of steps before the woman was again in the alley, her shadow chasing hers. "Here. It's just going to get thrown away." Emily never turned; the brown bag extended to her. She quickly grabbed it.

"Thank you…" Emily replied without turning. She could feel the young woman back away as Emily walked forward. The other woman's heartbeat never changed, nor did her breathing. No fear or judgment was coming from her, only kindness.

Emily tucked the brown bag into her sweatshirt before quickly moving through the streets. She didn't look at any of the people she passed. She could hear the remarks, the grumbles under their voices. She sped up until she was out of town, slipping onto the trail where she'd come into the community.

Emily raised her head, running her hands through her cut hair. It was such a small thing to wish for it to be cut and washed. She was never brave enough to cut her hair this short. The red hair was so uniquely her where she grew up. She was the only redhead in her class; there were times she was the only one in the school. She lifted her leg, placing her dirty, scuffed boot against the door of the booth. She had forgotten where she was for a moment. The brown paper bag was still in hand, and crumbs from the turkey sandwich were still on her lap.

"Forgive me, Father. It has been… days since my last confession."

She was sitting in the confessional, where she had taken refuge to eat lunch. It was the second time in several days she had come to recant the same confession hoping for her salvation.

"I have killed…" She had not allowed the wolf out since that night, since Colin. The wolf wanted out again the night before at the gas station.

"I'm not… I don't know what I'm doing here." She tried working through her thoughts. "I don't know if there is anything you or any god can do for me. I'm not sure what I believe anymore."

She reached for her neck, and memories of her youth when she went to Bible camp and was eager to go to Sunday school each week came back to her. The little silver cross given to her by her grandmother, she wondered what happened to the cross as she had left it behind in West Virginia with so much more.

"I'm not sure why any god would let this happen to anyone." Her vision blurred as she glanced away from her. "To me…" She could hear the wind shift under her door and through the booth next to her. "I'm not sure where I go from here."

She brought her boot down to the floor with a thud, feeling like a toddler wanting to throw a tantrum for not getting her way as she let her fall against the wall and took in a long deep breath before she stood and exited the booth into the main part of the church. She had been on the road for days, running out of money from the truck stop job she had worked for a few weeks in Nebraska. It wasn't a bad place to work, though she'd spent Christmas there in the small pay-by-the-week motel that wasn't much fit for anyone. She could have stayed there, but a regular had taken an aggressive liking to her. She didn't want to ask Ashley for more money, though she knew her best friend would have gladly sent her some.

Emily looked around the abandoned church. Most of the rows of chairs were rotted, and others were destroyed by partiers. There was a hole in the roof where a tree had crashed into it, and vines had taken over the floor. She had been looking for someplace off the road to sleep, to chain herself to a tree, and she stumbled upon the church. It looked like it had been years since it had hosted any congregation. She was just as happy to find it had a small basement with concrete floors which had been used as a pantry; all that was left from those days were broken jars.

Emily crossed the room to the back of the stage, where she had imagined the priest conducting his sermon. She was amazed the cross was still there and standing strong through its exposure to the elements. *Why did they leave and relocate?* she wondered. There had been a story there she would have been interested in once upon a time.

She sat down on the sleeping bag, the same spot she had nested and slept for the nights she stayed there. She pulled the dark fleece blanket up over her as she laid back, looking up at the ceiling. She could see holes in the roof, and nights in Oregon were much colder than in West Virginia this time of the year. She twisted, snuggling her nose into the flannel shirt and taking a long deep breath. She hadn't worn it since the night she'd spent with Colin. More so than the sweatshirt, it still smelled like her best friend that she had lost.

There was a creak of something stepping on the wood that caught her attention, followed by a sigh and a male's voice breaking the silence. "Hello?"

"Sheriff's Department. If you're here, please make yourself visible." There was a hint of frustration mixed with excitement in his voice as he groaned again when the old wood screamed under his carefully placed boot.

Emily rolled over to where she was clearly behind the stage, the blanket still with her. She could hear his boots as they approached now, even without the old wood. She gritted her teeth through her own frustration, having not heard him until he was already inside the old church. She could smell another, circling the back of the church. There was no quick escape from her where she wouldn't be seen.

"This place isn't safe." His voice was stern, and she imagined an older man. "Make it easier on yourself. Let me see your hands."

Emily took a long deep breath as she stood holding her hands up into the air. He was an older man in his late fifties, his firearm drawn and pointed in her direction.

"You alone?"

Emily nodded yes.

"It'll be easier if you don't lie to me." He came closer to her. She could see his jeans and thick boots. He wore a wool jacket over a flannel shirt. His head was shaven clean that morning. She could still smell the soap and shaving cream, and his face was just as clean-shaven except for a neat thick goatee. Thick glasses covered his eyes, but she could see the light brown of them and how they shifted around, looking to see if she was telling the truth. He didn't stop until he reached the back and looked down at her sleeping bag and blanket.

"You're a long way from West Virginia, missy…" She looked shocked when he said West Virginia. "I saw the plates on your truck."

He lowered his gun, and she exhaled when he did. He kept it at a ready as he looked around, approaching her. "Turn around, please." Emily did. She looked across the room. "Any weapons or open blades or needles I can cut myself on?"

"No, sir." He patted her down before finishing and stepping back away.

"There are laws against squatting, miss." She stood, shaking from her nerves. "Turn back around." She did and saw he had put his weapon back in its holster, his hands still resting on his hips as he looked down at the sleeping bag. "What's your name?"

"Sarah Jenkins," she lied. The real Sarah Jenkins was someone she had graduated from high school with, but had fallen off the radar to most of her classmates over the years.

"How long have you been sleeping up here, Ms. Jenkins?" he questioned.

"A few days, sir," she replied. She watched him twitch.

"A couple of hunters saw your truck, thought it looked suspicious and called it in." The man grimaced, looking around. "If I call this in, are you going to come back as some wanted fugitive, Ms. Jenkins?"

"No, sir," she replied.

He smiled. She knew it was the suspected answer anyone would have given him.

"You look a little old to be a runaway," he judged. "And a little too healthy for a junkie… An abusive husband or father you are running from?"

"I can leave, sir. I didn't mean to do any harm."

"You have any identification?" Emily dug into her back pocket. Her heart raced as she pulled the fake driver's license out and handed it over. She watched him look it over, back to her, and then to the card in his hand before he handed it back to her. "If you don't care to follow me into town, we'll get this whole misunderstanding taken care of. Maybe even get you a hot meal."

Emily nodded as she quickly gathered her belongings. As they stepped outside, the other man, with his weapon drawn, stepped out around the corner. "Put your gun away," the sheriff said, and the deputy obeyed. The other police officer said nothing as he got in the passenger side of the vehicle.

The entire trip into town, she had thought about leaving but didn't. Her anxiety got worse as they pulled into the sheriff's department. Emily pulled into space beside the sheriff, her hands on the steering wheel. She watched him exit his car, putting the cowboy hat back on his shaved head. He smiled. "If you don't mind, Miss Jenkins, just step inside for a minute."

Emily looked at the small police station. It looked no bigger than a fast-food restaurant. "Am I under arrest?"

"No," he replied, opening her door. She grabbed the door, stopping its progress. She could see the tension grow on his face as he looked at her hand. He spoke when their eyes met. "You can grab a shower and freshen up while I make some calls. You're not under arrest. And I'm Sheriff Banks."

Emily released her grip on the door. The officer smiled as she stepped out, she never even thought about putting on her seat belt, and she could see his gaze closed on the belt. The thought of a warm shower was enough to convince her to get out of the vehicle. Emily followed him in and watched him place his hat on the rack inside the door.

"Deputy Kerry, show Miss Jenkins to the shower." The deputy was close to her age, her dark hair pulled back into a ponytail. The uniform did nothing for her thin frame. Emily followed her down a dark-colored hallway until the end.

"Here you go." Emily could see the pity and disgust in the woman's expression as she opened the door. Emily didn't hesitate, stepping inside the concrete bathroom and closing the door behind her.

She sat on the bench, looking at the showers. She took a deep breath as she stood, gently removing her clothing before stepping in. She stood there inside the concrete cell; she knew it was used for prisoners as well as deputies. The showerhead sprayed scalding hot water over her soapy body. She never considered leaving until the water went from hot to warm to ice cold.

Emily stepped back out of the shower; her clothing was gone. She looked around, gasping in a panic as she saw the white t-shirt and running shorts sitting just inside the door. She quickly dried off before putting them on. She wanted to take another shower. The clothes clung to her body, a couple of sizes too big for her frame. She stepped out into the hall, bare feet on the cold floor. The air was just as frigid on her wet skin. She couldn't remember the last time she felt this clean.

She strolled down the hall, stopping close to the end, hearing the sheriff's voice. "So, is she one of yours?" His voice was filled with curiosity. "I called the Blackfoot reservation. I knew she wasn't from the res, but I wanted to cover all my bases beforehand. You were my next call…"

Emily stepped out into the open. She'd hoped he wasn't looking. The deputy and sheriff both spotted her about the same time. "Get the poor girl a jacket," the sheriff said with a wave of his hand. The deputy did as she was ordered. The male deputy from the church was nowhere to be seen.

"Feel better, honey?" she questioned, wrapping the thin, orange-colored jacket around Emily's shoulders.

"Much," Emily replied, pulling it close around her and covering her chest. She felt exposed as the thin clothes clung to her body.

"I put your clothes in a bag near the door." Emily glanced toward the door and back to the deputy.

"Thank you."

"Your story checks out, Sarah. Well, from what I could find, anyways," the sheriff said. He turned, leaning against his desk, giving her a questioning glare. He didn't get the answers he was looking for.

"I am sorry to be such trouble," Emily said.

"No trouble at all." He proclaimed with a smile. "You know, if you're planning on staying in town a while, you'll need someplace to stay besides that old church."

"I don't…"

"Rosie's over on main. I know the owner. She is always looking for more help, and with the spring season coming, she probably wouldn't mind having a pretty young woman such as you on her staff…who knows, maybe she might have a lead on a place to lay that head of yours for a while if you are looking for such a thing." The sheriff turned his back as he put his hat on.

Emily could only think about the wilderness. The vast expanse of wilderness and open territory within a short running distance… Maybe she could let the human side of her have a life. Her fake identification had been enough to get by the sheriff… She didn't know how Ashley managed it, but it had at least past the sheriff's inspection.

"What do you say?" the sheriff questioned.

She broke from her thoughts and shook her head feverishly yes to his question, like a child just being offered ice cream after a major disappointment.

Chapter Three

Emily lost track of time as she observed Sheriff Banks from the booth. He was outside talking to someone. The man reminded her of an old school principal who was easier on people than he should have been. He nodded his head once more before getting into his sheriff's jeep and driving off. Emily smiled as she stared at her reflection in the window. It wasn't until the click of the plate on the table did she turn back to see a server. "I didn't order anything…"

"The sheriff did. He assumed you weren't vegan or anything when he ordered." The woman was tall. She seemed to tower over Emily as she stood next to the table. "Can I get you a drink?" Emily looked around, the server from the alley earlier was gone from sight, but she could still smell her.

Emily lost herself staring at the burger and fries, biting her lower lip. "We have amazing lemonade." She looked back at the woman. "I can even give it a little extra kick if you need it, love."

"Yes, to just regular lemonade, please," Emily replied, watching the woman walk away. She immediately took a bite of the burger savoring the taste. She was on her second bite when the server returned, placing the lemonade at her side.

"Sarah Jenkins?"

Emily looked up at the older woman sitting across from her and nodded. Emily hadn't even realized someone else had sat at the booth. She was lost in the burger. "I'm Rosie. The sheriff seemed to think you could use a job." Emily nodded, still paying more attention to the burger.

"This is Meara." Emily's eyes shot up as the other woman appeared from the back. Her heart raced. "She has a small house not far outside of town and is looking for a roommate. The sheriff also seemed to indicate you need a place to live and that your background check came back all good."

Emily placed a hand in front of her mouth as she chewed. She knew there was no way the sheriff had time to run a proper background check on her. "Yes," Emily replied. She felt her stomach growl for more food, she knew how she looked like she hadn't eaten in weeks, and it felt much the same. She flushed with embarrassment as both women heard the unsettling of her stomach. "I'm sorry."

"Nothing to apologize for," Meara quickly declared. The woman had a confident, loving smile, but it didn't dominate her face. Her skin was pale; she wore dark eye shadow and extended lashes, but Emily found herself looking at her hair. Shoulder-length, dyed as white as snow, with only a few blonde streaks to highlight, no doubt her natural color. She had looked blonder when she had seen her outback of the restaurant.

"Why don't you finish your meal? Meara, you can take the rest of the day off and help Sarah get settled," Rosie said. "You start work tomorrow." Rosie looked to Meara. "I trust you will help her get in, work with you tomorrow and show her the routine." The older woman scooted out of her booth.

It wasn't until now Emily realized what she had agreed to as the other took a seat. The idea of sleeping in a warm bed was mostly on her mind now as she quickly finished her meal.

Emily paused, pulling her truck into the drive, watching the other woman get out of her beat-up Volkswagen Beetle with the flowered peace sign in the back glass. The car said a lot about the other woman and what Emily expected her to be like. The car was old but colorful, but even to Emily's untrained eye, she could tell where it had been patched up several times. The house looked smaller than her rented home back in West Virginia. The drive was rough and in need of fresh pavement. There were only two visible windows in the front of the old, color-faded brick house.

"It's not much, I know, but it has a roof over our head, and there are times that is really all you can ask for," Meara said as Emily stepped out of her truck. She knew this was a mistake. The other woman was quick to pull one of Emily's two bags from the back of her truck.

"We only have one neighbor." She pointed the opposite way they had driven in. "I'll warn you, they can be nosey and quite pushy if the wife catches you even the slightest bit bored or if you even look like you're looking for something to do. In the year I've lived here, she has asked me over at least a dozen times for one thing or another."

"Have you ever gone over to their place?" Emily asked out of curiosity.

"Hell no," Meara replied with a big smile. The other woman was a touch shorter, in her early twenties. She'd not noticed her dimpled smile or her clear brown eyes before.

"They're too uptight to be swingers or the sort that would approve of me on a normal day unless they are really good at hiding their more deviant side."

Emily paused. She watched the woman hoping for some sort of smile or hint that she was joking, but there was nothing of the sort. It wasn't until she reached the door and set the bag down did Emily rush to catch up with her. She was again standing at her side as she finished unlocking the third lock on the entrance. "The door sticks from time to time." She gave a small nudge with her shoulder into the door, and Emily followed her inside. "Two bedrooms, on opposite ends." Meara pointed in the direction of each. One bedroom was opposite the living room. Meara pointed back toward the kitchen, "That one is mine, so…" She dragged Emily's bag off to the one near the living room. "One bathroom also, kitchen and living room, basically one room… It's all small, but…"

"It's a roof." Emily smiled. She considered it was much better than the old church or even the motel she had stayed in Nebraska.

Emily entered the room, and there was no doubt it was bare, only a bed and no other furniture in the room. Emily sat her bags on the bed. "There is a linen closet in the bathroom. I have some extra sheets there." Emily followed the woman out. "And here is the best thing…" Emily stepped out the back door behind the other woman, there was a large backyard, and Emily could only think about sleeping in the bed. "There is a lake, about a half-mile that way." Meara pointed. "Well, they call it a lake. It isn't that big, but it has a clear trail most of the way around it. It's good if you're a runner." Emily smiled without even realizing it, and it didn't go unnoticed by Meara. "You look like you're a runner. I will warn you, though, this time of the year, the water if frigid and not much for swimming, but it is beautiful to look at."

"I used to be a runner," Emily replied, feeling her face flush. She wasn't sure if it was excitement or embarrassment, but the idea of going for a run for no other reason except to run excited her.

"I'm not." Meara smiled, walking past her back into the home, and Emily followed. Emily turned, and Meara turned, walking backward. "Just, if you do, be careful. There has been a black bear spotted around the lake recently. Just coming out due to the warmer days, so he may be a little testy, but mostly harmless."

"Why are you doing this?" Emily paused, stopping in her tracks. Meara stopped and smiled. "You don't know me… why do this for me?"

"It was you in the alley this morning," Meara said. "I've been in your situation, not knowing when my next meal would be… it's a hopelessness one can't understand unless you've been there."

"You're trusting a stranger," Emily muttered, her eyes watered on the edge of tears as she looked to the floor.

"Look, darling, I'm trusting you because I believe there is a better chance. You're a decent human being who is just going through a rough spell," Meara replied. There was no judgment in the girl's motives, she truly just wanted to help, and Emily could focus on her heartbeat to know she was being truthful. "And not some sort of wild animal, serial killer, or something else."

Emily's new roommate was gone not an hour after they arrived. She was still having difficulty understanding why the sheriff, Rosie, and Meara were being so friendly. Meara, she could almost understand. She was getting a very loving, hippie vibe from the woman. She thought the girl reminded her of Ashley, just without the forceful attitude and caring for a stranger. Ashley was loving, but only to her friends. The more she compared, the less she considered them to be alike. Ashley would have hated the peace and love attitude. The sheriff, he should have been able to see through the ruse. The ID wasn't that good. She opened the other girl's bedroom door. It didn't take a moment to see the large peace sign, like the one in her back glass hanging just inside the door, reaffirming her opinion of Meara. She quickly closed the door, not wanting to be nosey. She didn't want to get caught snooping. She crossed, finding the back door of the house, stepping outside, and feeling the instant frigid air.

Emily was still in the clothing from the police station, minus the jacket. She walked barefoot across the yard, not stopping until she reached the edge of the woods. It was thick, and lots of trees had fallen, but it wasn't hard to find the path used by deer to eat in the grass. She walked on, paying little attention to where she stepped. Dried leaves and kindling snapped under each step. She could smell the lake water and feel the cold breeze whispering through the forest.

Emily never stopped as she slipped through the woods, one muddy step after another. Not stopping until she reached the lake. She could imagine it frozen as kids, teenagers, and those youthful skating across the lake during the coldest of winters. She stepped into the water. She knew it was cold, but she could barely feel it. She never stopped. As the chilly water overtook her form, every curve until there was nothing solid under her step, and she floated, looking up at the sky, drifting off into unconsciousness.

Emily was soaked when she came through the back door, her clothes clinging to her.

"I am beginning to wonder if you're housebroken."

Emily gasped.

"I'm joking." Meara was sitting at the kitchen table. Emily faked a shiver as the other woman crossed the room, retrieving a lavender towel for her to dry off with. "You've been gone a while. I was beginning to think you ran off."

"Like a stray?" Emily smirked.

Meara smiled. "I guess. I have a habit, don't I? I dried your clothes and put them in your room."

Emily had not realized she'd been gone so long. "Thank you."

"I'm going to bed. You're welcome to anything in the fridge." The girl turned and walked toward her. "This is yours…" The woman handed her a phone. "I'm sure there is someone out there worried about you. Don't worry. It's a burner, but it'll allow you to reach out to anyone who is missing you." The younger woman stopped at the door. "We all have secrets." She disappeared.

Emily flipped the old phone open, and there was already one call placed on it under the title "Meara".

Emily woke the next morning, unsure of when she went to sleep the night before. She rolled over and could see light peeking through the window as she took a long deep breath. She glanced at her phone. It wouldn't be long before she would have to be at work, but the thought of doing something normal crossed her mind. It had been a long time, but she ached for a run. A real run, not like the few nights before when she was trying to get away from the gas station.

Emily picked up her pace as she placed the headphones in her ears, though there was no music. She felt the most alive now, the most like her former self when she ran. She had done her stretching and kept track of her pulse as she entered the first mile of her run. When she reached the lake, it took her breath away. The lake looked like glass in the cold light of morning. She took to the path the same as the night before, not expecting to see anyone except a fisherman. She knew if any saw her out here running, they would think she was crazy, especially with the large smile she couldn't contain. It was a small incline. She picked up the pace, feeling the burn in her legs until she topped the embankment and stopped. She took a deep breath, and the cold air burned. It was so cold here this time of the year compared to West Virginia; it was a different world. The wilderness was vaster and dangerous.

Emily heard the crack of a limb. Quickly, she turned and saw it. Mist flowed from its nostrils. It watched with eager curiosity, and the bear was well fed. Its black fur bristled, soaked from the lake, and she could see the cool touch of frost on it. It watched her closely and even took a step backward as their eyes met. It knew who the real predator was.

"Go away," she mumbled, and the bear was quick to do as it was told. Emily smiled.

She continued her run, not until she rushed through the door of the home. She locked it behind her being careful to secure the deadbolts. It was more than her aggression she tried to work out. She had wanted to tire herself. It had been a couple of months since she had spent any time with people, and today was her first day at a new job.

Chapter Four

Emily parked her truck next to Meara's car, and she took a deep breath. She knew nothing more than assumptions about the other woman, but she was glad she was there on her first day. She exited the door just as another car pulled in beside her. The car was beaten up, and there was a miss in the engine as it came to a stop. A woman near Emily's age got out, wearing jeans and a pullover shirt. "You must be Sarah…"

Emily watched her with a hint of confusion as she nodded. "I'm Allison." Emily could smell the scent of a kid on her. "It's Friday. I figure I should warn you before you go in. It's the one day of the week our job is difficult. All the logging companies cater on Friday, and we deliver their meals." The woman grabbed her shirt from the back seat, putting it on. "And it's our busiest day of the week even without the catering."

The two of them entered the backdoor immediately, seeing another server. "You're late," she growled. Emily wanted to growl back but didn't. The woman was twenty at the most and smelled of sex, but she realized she was looking at Allison. There was also a familiar lavender scent mixed with oil exuding from the woman. Emily recognized the younger woman. It was the girl from the gas station a couple nights before. It was just as obvious to Emily that she did not recognize her.

Emily did not reply. She walked past the younger woman with a few quick steps, getting an even nastier look from her as she went. "This the new girl?"

"Yes," she heard Allison reply.

"Not much of a talker, are you?" Emily watched as the much younger woman looked her up and down, and still, she could see she had no recollection of who she was looking at.

She never looked back, but she could hear the other woman sigh and grumble under her breath. "Stop being a bitch, Chloe." Emily didn't turn around. She could hear the gasp in Chloe's breath.

"You can't talk to me like that," Chloe quickly said. "I'll tell Rosie…"

"And Rosie will tell you, stop being a bitch," the third woman quickly said with a hint of laughter. Chloe stormed out of the room, and Emily turned around. Allison disappeared into the front. Meara appeared from the diner. "You were gone early this morning. I didn't realize I was rooming with a morning person." Emily could see the other woman had not been awake for long.

"I hope I didn't wake you. I was aching for a run," Emily replied as she nervously climbed the small set of steps into the diner.

"I can sleep through almost anything," Meara replied, removing her shirt and Emily found herself admiring the art. She had at least half a dozen tattoos from her shoulders to the waistline on her back. Meara caught her. "You have any?"

"Not my thing," Emily said, turning away. She could hear a chuckle in Meara's breath. She had wanted to say something else. Emily turned, and she could see at least three other tattoos on her stomach, chest, and shoulder.

"There is this bonfire tomorrow night when most of the town will be out watching the precious final football game. Us heathens will be there… you should think about coming along," Meara said. Emily watched her button up her lite blue blouse. "I'll introduce you to some of the more fun people in the area."

Meara had a wicked smile, and Emily was noticing. "I'll think about it," Emily replied, remembering the conversation about the neighbors not being deviants. "How many?"

"Tattoos?" Meara replied with a big smile. "Thirteen." Emily watched her turn back as she shut her locker door. "All hidden where I can still pretend to be a good little girl when I want to be," she said with a wink. Meara once again reminded her of Ashley, or maybe more than ever, she was beginning to realize how much she missed her best friend. "And my father doesn't have to explain my evil ways to the local minister."

"What about that one?" Meara paused, looking down at her exposed cleavage and the small pentagram.

Meara smiled big as she looked back. "Are you going to ask if it means I worship the devil?"

"No…" Emily paused. It would have meant as much to most of the church-going people she had grown up with, her dad included.

"It's a representation of my faith. I'm a practicing Pagan; it is such a common misconception. The pentagram has nothing to do with Satanism or worshipping the devil." Meara smiled as she began to point to each point of the star. "Spirit, water, fire, earth, and air, it represents all that is life." Emily was unsure if she had ever seen anyone smile as big as the young woman across from her. Her smile seemed to light up the entire room.

Emily was puzzled. "A witch?"

"Pagan… not witchcraft." Meara crossed the room, placing a hand on Emily's chest where her heart would be. "It means I am more about the heart and love. Loving one another, and I don't mean orgies out in the forest around roaring fires, if you're worried that is what I'm inviting you to. It's about love… though the orgies can be quite fun, that's more for those warm springs and fall nights…" Meara winked.

Emily felt like she was blushing. She thought Meara was joking but wasn't completely sure.

Meara continued to smile, removing her hand. She always was smiling. "It means I am about treating every person, animal, and being on mother earth with love." She finished buttoning up her shirt.

Emily turned to see Chloe with her dissatisfied look watching the two of them. "We could use a little help on the floor, you know." She turned and disappeared back into the waiting room.

"Little snot," Meara said. Emily smiled as she went to start her day. Emily took a long deep breath before walking through the doors into the diner.

Emily's day went by quickly, with little frustration, less than she expected, but she knew she needed a release. She pulled into the drive of the home just as Meara shut the trunk of her car. "You want to come with?"

Emily hesitated, and the woman smiled big. "I don't bite. We're going to live together. You should learn a little more about me… and my faith. Or my representation of it. And well, this will let me learn more about you." The woman was dressed in jogging pants and a pullover hoodie. It wasn't the look she expected her to have. "Like all religions, we all have our interpretation which is always a little different from the next person."

Emily forced a smile. It wasn't that she was nervous about learning more about her new roommate. She was deathly afraid of Meara learning things about her that she desperately wanted to keep secret.

Emily rode along thirty minutes until they got to a sign saying no trespassing. "Where are we going?" Meara had parked off to the side of the road, and she was quick to exit the vehicle heading to the back. She didn't know what to expect when she looked in the trunk, but the small five Bruce saplings weren't it.

"There are three logging companies here in Oakridge. Two of them are particularly good about replanting trees after they leave an area. Bell Logging isn't one of them. Which is more infuriating considering the patriarch was labeled a naturalist… believe that is just because of his affection for nudity and not his love of nature." Meara pointed to the sign, and Emily could see the initials "BL". The two of them hiked nearly a mile past the gate, careful to stay off the road. They came to the edge of a clearing when Meara pulled out a small shovel and began to dig.

They had planted a dozen trees before they returned home, and Meara didn't stay long before she left again. Emily would admit the afternoon had given her more of a rush than she was expecting, but it wasn't the excitement she wished for. She had waited till the edge of dark before she pulled her hoodie on and slipped out into the cool air. It was ten miles to the church through the wilderness; it was pitch-black when she finally found her way inside. Through the old doors into the basement, she dug the bag out of the rubble where she had hidden it. She was thankful Sheriff Banks and the deputy hadn't searched the church grounds. She wouldn't have been able to explain the bag full of chains and padlocks. The room was dark and mostly empty except for the table and chains. Securely latched to the cold concrete floor, she approached. She had to do it tonight. There was no more waiting. She could not take the chance of another incident like at the gas station. She quickly undressed, placing all her clothing on the table before she approached her prison for the night.

Emily's head pounded. With each buzz of the alarm, her eyes felt like they were about to burst into tears from the headache. She could see the time through her foggy vision and knew it would be daylight in a couple of hours. She had not allowed the change. Sitting up, she fought with the cuff until she was able to toss it aside. The concrete was freezing, but it did not matter. Her skin boiled with a fever. She ached. Why couldn't she change? She knew tonight she would have to try again. She grabbed the shirt from the table and quickly dressed as she rushed up the stairs. Just one night in a warm home, and she had forgotten how cold the church was in the morning and it sent goose pimples across her body. Or it was the touch of her skin was boiling.

She was just entering the back door of the home as the sun was trying to open the curtains casting shadows into the room. The bathroom was tiny. The sink next to the toilet and the bathtub and shower behind her was it. She splashed cold water onto her face as she glared into her own eyes.

"Pull it together." She forced a smile. She knew this was going to be a long day, it would be a full moon tonight, and the change would come easier. She could feel it even now as she questioned her reasons for not allowing it the night before. She didn't understand why she didn't allow it; something in her subconscious. The wolf just would not present itself. She tossed the shirt from her body and into the basket, quick to freshen up in the shower.

Most of the day had gone, and it was near closing. Emily had gotten cornered. Two servers had not shown up for their evening shift. Meara was quick to volunteer, but Emily was not. She was left with little choice when Chloe left, leaving her to take the other shift. It had been dark for an hour when the rush died. Emily sat out back with a cigarette in her fingers. She wasn't lost in her thoughts. She was trying extremely hard to keep it together. She had pushed it for too long, and she could feel the anger grow in her stomach. There was nothing specific she was mad at, just herself. Just the fact the wolf wanted out, and she was someplace with people, and she could not let go.

"Almost over," she heard Meara state as she stepped out into the cool night air. "You have another of those?" Emily never spoke as she picked up the half-emptied pack and handed it over. She found it calmed the nerves. "I needed this before I went off and killed someone." Emily smiled, looking back at the other woman. "I didn't know you smoked."

"Only on occasion," Emily replied, turning back to her staring contest with the cat as it picked at some scraps. "Do you practice any sort..." The cat kept its eyes on Emily while it ate. Emily leaned forward, hissing, and backed away. Emily couldn't help but smile.

"Magic?" Meara said with a laugh.

"No... yes, I was trying to figure a better way of saying it. I mean, magic isn't real..." *But werewolves are*, she wanted to say. How far of a stretch was it to believe witches were?

"For me, it's more about finding peace," Meara said, taking a seat beside her. "Meditation, controlling one's aura, basically becoming connected with who you are meant to be without the aid of unnatural influences." Emily looked at the cigarette between the woman's fingers. "Oh, I didn't say I was perfect."

But something else caught her eye: a small tattoo on her wrist peeking out from under her shirt. "Is that a crow?" Emily smiled as she watched her expose the small black crow on her wrist.

"Good eye," Meara replied.

"A friend of mine had one, a big one on her back." Emily could almost remember the day Ashley had gotten it and how she had backed out of getting one of her own. It wasn't that she had any fear of the pain. It was more she had no clue what she wanted to have tattooed on her body for the rest of her life.

"Had?" Meara questioned with a hint of sorrow.

Emily smiled as she took a drag off the cigarette. "We're not in each other's lives anymore." She thought about the dream from the church and how Lauren spoke about the crow being a vessel of transformation. This was all too much. She thought about Ashley's tattoo as well. For a moment, she wondered if there was some greater power at work, and whether she was meant to meet her new white-haired friend.

They heard a ruckus coming from inside, and they quickly went to investigate. There had only been a few customers inside when they took their break, easy enough for one server to handle. Allison was on the floor, just beginning to crawl away. The man towered over her three times her size.

"Call the police." Emily quickly started circling to Allison's side.

"Bitch," the man said in a growl between huffs of anger.

"Just go," Emily said. The man had not even looked at her until now. Allison held her mouth where he had hit her. "The police are on the way." The man just laughed. Emily helped her coworker to her feet and pulled her away, putting her own body between her and the man.

"You little bitch, this has nothing to do with you." Emily surveyed the rest of the dining area. Only an elderly couple remained, the man had started to stand, but he needed the assistance of a cane.

"Just go, sleep it off." Emily felt Allison's hand grab her own tightly. Another feeling took control, her stomach churned as the man took a step forward. Emily put a handout in front of her, and the man slapped it away with a laugh.

"You can't stop me," he said with a thunderous laugh.

She could. Just not with others around, and she wanted too very badly. "Just don't." He took a couple of steps forward and close enough now, closer than she wished.

"What are you going to do, little girl?" he said.

Emily growled. It was a loud, intense sound, and everyone heard it.

The man only chuckled. "Amusing little trick. Is this the bitch you've been seeing, Allie? Have you gone full dyke on me? God will judge you both for your sins."

He went to smack Emily, but she stopped his progress with her hand, he was nearly twice her size, and he had gone to hit her hard, but still, she had no problem stopping him. Emily forcefully lifted her knee into the man's stomach, knocking him backward to the ground.

The man was quickly back on his feet, looking at Emily. She could see the anger on his face. Flushed with embarrassment, Emily took a few steps backward, pushing Allison away and to the floor in the process. Her stomach seized; she could feel the spasms. The wolf wanted out. The wolf wanted to take care of this man.

The man laughed loudly, "Must be your time of the month." Emily looked up, she knew her eyes had changed, and he had seen them immediately. "What the hell?"

"You need to leave," Emily said. Her voice was hoarse, and it was a growl. The man did not take the threat lightly. He quickly stepped toward her. Emily closed her eyes and waited. The hit came fast, the left side of her head, but it only felt like a stung as she fell to her hands and knees. The hit never hurt, but she could feel all her muscles tighten and strengthen as she closed her eyes, taking a few quick breaths. She could hear him laugh. He thought he had won. Again, she growled. She tried to keep it as quiet as possible, trying to regain her senses and keep the wolf down.

She opened her eyes; her vision was clear. She slowly stood, showing no sign of where he had hit her. He took a step backward but continued to laugh. "Little girl thinks she's tough."

It was then she saw the two men by the door. He was talking to them. She realized who they were: the men she assaulted at the gas station, but neither had recognized her. Much like Chloe, she wondered if a shower and a change of clothing had profoundly changed her appearance so much that she was unrecognizable to them.

The sirens began to fill the room, and the police officers quickly entered. Emily whirled until she was leaning into the counter. She could hear people talking. Voices were all a blur as she let her weight on the counter, feeling the pain shoot through her body. Her eyes closed, and she breathed.

"Sarah!" She opened her eyes, looking up at Meara standing on the other side of the counter. She took a moment to look around. A police officer was talking to the old couple. An EMT stood beside her, he had been the one talking to her, but she never heard a word he had said.

"I'm all right," she said. "I'm all right."

"I'm closing up early and taking you home," she heard Meara say.

Meara insisted, helping her into her car and driving her to their shared home. Emily didn't argue. She knew she couldn't take the time. She had told the other woman she was going straight to bed. Instead, she had thrown her hoodie on and crawled out the small window. She was frantic. It took half the night for her to reach the church. She stumbled along the way; she tripped over her feet several times as she ran. She began to take her clothes off as she reached the door. Her shirt, bra, then shoes, pants, and panties. She had just reached the wall when she felt the pain in her stomach worsen. She felt her canines grow. There was going to be no fighting it this night. She knew she was lucky she had not changed in the diner, let alone made it to the church. She latched the chain on her ankle just before she felt all her muscles spasm, foam, and drool from her mouth. She knew she had held it off too long, and it was her body adjusting to the infrequency. Her body arched off the floor before she rolled over onto her stomach. One more chain. She pulled forward until it was within reach, and the pain was becoming unbearable as she latched the final cuff onto her wrist.

Chapter Five

Emily knew the taste in her mouth. Her eyes were blurry and dry. She had been crying for hours in her sleep. Every muscle in her body ached, rolling over onto her back, but her right arm immediately ceased to move as the chain halted her progress. She glanced at her wrist; it was red. The scratches were evident where the other had fought hard against the cuff the night before. She sat up, entering the combination on the lock as it fell from her wrist. She looked to her ankle at a similar bracelet and chain; she quickly removed the lock. After both were free, she lay back on her back to the cold concrete, but it didn't seem to bother her as she stretched out. She had lain quietly for thirty minutes when the alarm on her phone across the room began to chime, startling her from her rest. She rolled over, sat up on her knees, looking at the floor. She could only smile at the deep scratches on the concrete floor as she thought about how hard the other part of her fought against the bindings, wanting a taste of freedom. Something she knew she could not let the wolf have, not until she had more control. She was conscious during it all, but it felt like a dream.

She stood, walking to the table and quickly putting her clothes on. She was off today, and after the night before, she knew she needed to not be in a rush to get back home, though she fully expected Meara would want to come to check on her. It never mattered if it was a full moon, it was a myth. She knew the feeling was at its worst on nights of the full moon. The hunger was always there, the need to run in the wilderness. The need to hunt.

She strolled up the stairs out into the abandoned church for her run home. She had slipped back into the window she had escaped the night before. She listened, hearing only a light rumble from the other room. She grabbed the robe Meara had loaned her and quickly covered her muddy body as she unlocked the door heading out into the main living area.

"How are you feeling?" Meara sat with a book in front of her.

"I'm okay," she replied.

"Are you sure? I tried to check on you, but you had the door locked, and I swear I couldn't hear you make even a peep of sound while you slept," Meara questioned.

"I'm sure I'm fine," Emily replied.

"You took a nasty hit to the head, and I thought you were going to sleep all day. I was almost afraid you may have had a concussion," Meara said, and it was at this time the doorbell rang. "Fuck." Meara looked toward the door. "Um..." She slowly stood, walking to the door and then back to Emily. "Um, it's our neighbor... she is... cheerful and annoying." Meara opened the door, and Emily immediately noticed the woman on the other side with her bubbly smile. "Hey, Andrea."

"How many times do I have to tell you to call me Ann?" the woman questioned, almost bouncing as she stepped into the room. Emily glanced off toward the bathroom wanting nothing more than to escape the situation.

"What can I do for you, Ann?"

"I was curious if you heard anything last night?" the woman questioned. She was perky, always with the same full smile, and Emily could see it annoyed her roommate. Emily stepped into the bathroom, leaving the door open. She could hear them from the other room. More importantly, she could smell the other woman and intuitively knew she owned several pets. She turned the faucet on and splashed water into her face.

"What do you mean?" Meara questioned. Emily barely recognized the woman looking back at her in the mirror. She knew people were looking for her. There were missing person alerts and often the mention of her long flowing red hair.

Emily turned to step back out into the main room. "Oopsie." Emily turned to see the woman staring, and for a moment, she did not realize she was spilling out of her robe.

Emily pulled it tight around her. "I never heard anything last night." Emily looked to Meara. She knew she had changed a shade of red, and so did Andrea on seeing the other woman's breast. It made Meara smile.

"My dog Beaches just howled and howled all night long." She raised her hands, showing spirit fingers. Emily heard Meara groan. Meara was always cheerful, but something about their neighbor annoyed her new friend.

"I never heard or saw anything I crashed when I got home," Emily said, turning to look at the woman, pushing her best, most cheerful smile.

Andrea smiled. "I don't know what it is. She has been doing that a lot these past couple of days, keeping us up all night. I heard nothing either, but you know animals, their senses are more advanced than ours."

Emily smiled. "I have heard that." She walked past Andrea, giving another glance at the open door. "I need to change, if you'll give me a moment." She watched the woman smirk.

"We haven't met." She pushed her hand out in front of her, and Emily shook it, having been cut off from her approach to her room.

"That's Sarah," Meara said. "She is a friend from out of town. She'll be staying with me for a while." Emily rushed past her when the neighbor focused again on Meara. Emily quickly put on a sports bra and a shirt, dark running shorts, and shoes. She exited the room. She had hoped when she came from the room the other woman would be gone, but she found her in the kitchen sitting at the table across from Meara.

"Burton is having a cookout soon. There will be some of his friends and others from the community there… it'll be good for the two of you. I worry about you living here all by your lonesome… I never see anyone here." Emily frowned. "And I'm sure there will be some eligible bachelors."

"I will consider it," Meara replied.

"I'm going to go for a run." Emily stood, wanting to make a dash for the backdoor.

"You are going for a run? I wish I'd known. I would have gone with," Andrea said.

"I like going alone," Emily said.

"Be careful out there," Andrea said, Emily could hear the higher guttural tone to the woman's voice and her heart started to beat faster.

"I will see you later." Emily gave Meara a nod.

Emily ached. She wanted to finish it off. She wanted to leave herself completely exhausted, the run to the church, letting the wolf out, the return home, and now this. She wanted to feel weak, but with each passing step, it felt as if she was only getting more energy as her adrenaline pulsed through her. She was nearly a mile into her run when she stopped to enjoy the lake, but it was more. Something caught her eye. Red and blue lights flashed around the lake from her. She knew she should turn back, but she continued walking the trail. A moment later, she was back into a run. She watched the lights running further as she pulled the earbuds free. She slowed to a walk; the lights close now. She could hear people as they scurried around, bringing her to a stop. It wasn't until now she smelled it. Another like her. Another werewolf.

"Excuse me, ma'am." She turned. He scared her, her heart racing, and she knew how she looked like she was going to pounce. "I'm sorry to startle you."

She saw clearly by his light tan uniform and badge that he was a wildlife official, with short dirty blonde hair and just enough waves to make him look like he had stepped out of a shampoo ad. His beard was thick, and his blue eyes seemed glued to her own.

"What happened?" She turned to look back toward where Fish and Game officer's vehicle lights filtered through the forest.

"Black bear, ma'am," he said, stepping onto the trail and approaching her.

"Please don't call me ma'am." He smiled.

"I saw you at the diner, but I wasn't brave enough to catch your name." Emily didn't remember him, but her two shifts were mostly a blur, and she was happy to make it through them. Working at a diner made her miss her days working at a lawyer's office. It was one thing more obvious to her, not only did she feel more energized the morning after a turn, but she seemed to think and see much clearer without the ache of the restless wolf.

"Sarah," Emily replied. She had a tough time getting used to the first few months, but now she had become comfortable with using her alias.

"Don." He reached his hand out and shook it.

"What happened, Don?"

"We have a dead black bear, the thing was left in pretty bad shape," Don replied. "You run these trails often?"

"Not really." Emily smiled at him, she knew he was taking it as flirty, but she was happy to know the other werewolf had not killed a person. She had grown up in rural parts of West Virginia and Kentucky; reports of violence were rare, but she had found them even less so in rural Oregon. "What do you suppose happened?" She took a step forward, and he grabbed her quickly by the elbow.

"You don't want to see that, Sarah, trust me." Emily was sure she had seen and done much worse. He released his grip on her arm when she took a step back closer to him. "It's gruesome. I'm not sure if I'll ever not see it myself. If I were a guessing man, I'd say another bear did it. It was fairly ripped apart."

"Thank you," Emily replied, turning and walking down the trail back the way she had come.

She was only a few feet away. "Sarah?"

She turned, smiling, watching the man. "Yes?"

"Maybe next time I stop by the diner, I can buy you a cup of coffee?" he questioned, and she smiled.

"Sure." He was cute and rugged, so not her type, but she thought it was funny a man who looked at home in the outdoors would be so hesitant and timid about asking her to have coffee. "I work tomorrow." He smiled, running a hand through his perfect hair. Emily turned, running down the trail.

Emily never returned home. She found a spot on the opposite shore to watch the wildlife officials, but only when she could see all the vehicles had left did she return to her run. She moved faster than before, some eagerness in her pace as she came to where Don had interrupted her. She stopped looking around, seeing no one. She closed her eyes, listened, took the territory in, and then took a deep breath smelling the area. It had taken her a long time to get used to her enhanced senses, but she found them useful. She was sure there was no one there, but she caught the smell of something different. Death. Slowly, she walked forward. She could see by the ground where the men had trampled and taken the corpse of the black bear away. Her senses were being cruel. She could smell the corpse, but still, there was more. She could smell the other wolf as well. There was still more death in the air. She walked well on past the trail, near a quarter of a mile past where the bear had been found, and the smell was enough to make her mouth water involuntarily. She had tasted human flesh. She felt guilty every day for what she had done and often had nightmares about Detective Vance.

"Hello?" she muttered. She knew there was no one there to answer, but she said it.

She crept through the brush, vines, and briars ripping at her bare legs, but she had to see it. She could see the edge of the water now, but still nobody. The embankment was slick, and before she knew it, she was on her back in the silk mud.

"Damn it!" she called out, sitting up. No longer worrying about trying to stay clean, she slid down to the edge of the water, and she saw him there entangled in a tree. She could see where he had tried to claw his way out of the water using the tree. This man had lived through the attack, though she could not see how. The only wound she could see was on his face, four deep slashes down from his upper scalp to his cheek, and she could see bone through the cuts.

"Poor bastard." She didn't know the circumstances involving the other wolf, a bear, and the unlucky man she stared at.

Emily had not encountered another wolf since Lauren, and she was unsure if she wanted to know. She got to her feet and headed home. She had a lot to think about and some decisions to make. She would have nothing to worry about if the wolf was just passing through, but she had his scent now. She would know him instantly if she crossed him in his human form.

Chapter Six

Emily had spent the entirety of the night without sleep, thinking about the other wolf. Whether she should stay or run, the sheriff, Rosie, and Meara, all who had taken her in. She had hoped the other wolf was only passing through. But it had to have smelled her, she'd been at the lake the day before, and it wasn't a coincidence.

Rosie's Diner was the most popular during the day, with workers and kids skipping school for its burgers and shakes. Emily sat out back smoking her second cigarette, she hated the habit, but when her nerves and anxiety were at their highest, she indulged. It seemed to help calm the wolf.

"Sarah?"

She turned to see Rosie with her head popped out the window. "I know you're on your break, but a customer has requested you specifically. Something about a cup of coffee."

"Dirty blonde-haired ranger?" Emily smiled. He had come, just as he said. Now, what was she going to do? The day before, she was playing nice. This was before she knew about a human casualty.

"Yes." Rosie smiled. "Don Martin, I could give you the low down on him if you'd like, sweetie."

"I think I'd rather find out on my own." She smiled before carefully putting the cigarette out under her heel and disregarding the rest in the trash. The small town reminded her of home in another way after only a few days. Everybody knew everybody and everyone else's business whether they liked it or not. She pushed a piece of gum between her partially chapped lips before entering the back door of the diner. His wavy hair was easy to spot. After passing through the grill area, not stopping until she was in the dining room, she saw him instantly. "I never expected you to show."

"Well, when a beautiful woman asks you out on a date, it's hard to refuse." His smile was overconfident, but she could see his handshaking with a touch of nerves. But primarily, she could hear his heart thundering beneath his chest.

Emily smiled at Rosie as she poured the cup of coffee, but did not speak until she was gone. "I believe it was you who asked me out." She looked at his beard. It was graying, as were his eyes, and some of his once dark blonde roots were littered with graying hair. He was older than she thought, early to mid-forties.

"Where are you from, Sarah?"

"Kentucky." It was only partially a lie. A lot of her mother's family had originated from Pikeville, Kentucky. She was born there and lived there in her youth.

"Family?"

"Orphaned at an early age." Emily looked away, attempting to look sad. It was not a stretch. She had gone without seeing her parents for the longest time in her life. Or since she and Ashley had met.

"Sorry." Don took a sip of his coffee.

"You from here, Don?"

"Born and raised a few miles out of town." He smiled, sitting back in his chair. "Two older brothers, too, who to this day haven't let me forget how they used to save my butt from bullies."

"I have a tough time believing you were bullied." Emily smiled, taking a drink of her coffee.

"I was a scrawny kid," he replied with a smile. She replied with a smile of her own. She found his smile enduring and charming. She watched as he ran his hand through his hair and looked at his watch. It was easy to see he often did when he was nervous. "I'd like to take you out for a proper dinner."

Emily smiled. "How about I make you dinner? Tomorrow night."

"Hey Don, you there?"

The radio on the table beside Don buzzed into their conversation with a female voice. He at once picked it up, holding it to his mouth. Emily watched him wet his lips before he spoke. "Yeah, whatcha need, Bailey?"

"Sheriff needs you back out where they found that black bear yesterday."

"How come?"

"Never said. Just told you to hurry. He sounded like he was in shock."

"Thanks, Bailey." He clipped the radio back out of sight. Emily knew it was on his belt.

"What's going on?" She knew they had found the body.

"Don't know, but the sheriff freaks about any little thing." He stood pulling money for a tip from his pocket, and Emily stood in front of him. "So, tomorrow night?'

"It's a date." A full day and a half, plenty of time for her to make up her mind if it was time for her to pull up and leave town. Or pump the officer for information when he was at her place. Emily turned and watched as he left. She turned back, heading into the back to find Rosie waiting.

"Don Martin, huh?" Rosie smiled. "He is a nice guy, you could do worse. Trust me when I say nice guys around here can be far and between. And you should know, he has a daughter."

"Not an issue." Emily smiled. "You don't mind if I take the rest of the day off?"

With a nod, she said, "It's a slow day. We will be fine if you need to take off."

Emily wanted to go back to the lake, find other clues about the other wolf and find some way of tracking him. There was one thing she was almost positive about the scent left behind. It was a male. And the very fact she knew that left her twisting in her seat with an extreme uneasiness in her stomach. She pulled into the drive to find Meara waiting, knowing her plans would not happen. "So, you ready for our night out?"

"What?" Emily questioned.

"Camping," Meara said with a smile as she moved out of the way. Emily could see everything the younger woman had in her truck. "We missed the bonfire the other night, so I figure tonight is a good night to show you some of the nightlife. We could drive out to the hot springs, but I'm not sure you're ready for that. Clothing is optional… bet you didn't know Oregon was hippy central, did you?"

"I'm not sure tonight is a good night." Emily was focused on the other wolf.

"I'm going whether you go or not. Neither of us are working tomorrow, and I figured it would be a good night for us to get better acquainted," Meara replied.

Emily sighed. She couldn't let Meara go out there alone.

"Are you hungry?"

Emily opened her eyes and sat up without breathing. "Colin?"

"You look like you've seen a ghost." He smiled, dropping an armload of lumber on the ground.

Emily smiled.

"Cat got your tongue, Red?" Colin questioned, placing a couple of the logs into the fire. Emily leaped to her feet and into his arms. She felt his lips on her own, his arms tightly around her, holding her off the ground.

"I'm sorry," she whispered. She could still taste his lips.

"What for, Red?" She opened his eyes. His boyish grin was close enough that she could tell his lips were just beginning to chap. This felt real, the realest she had ever felt being held by another, but she knew it wasn't.

"I am sure there is something I owe you an apology for," she wanted to apologize for getting him killed. She could live in this dream forever.

"You're perfect." She felt her feet on the ground again. She smirked, wanting to remain there, lost in his arms. Safe.

Meara was meditating when Emily opened her eyes. She was unsure about the time, but half the night had passed as she looked around the looming darkness. This was her life now. Growing up a tomboy, she hated camping, but now, she was more at home in the wilderness. The other part of her, the wolf, was at home in the wilderness too.

"That was an exciting dream." Emily looked to Meara, who was smiling as wide as she thought humanly possible.

"Sorry…" Emily blushed. She could remember the dream quite vividly. "Was I talking in my sleep?"

"Not exactly talking." Meara gave her a wink. "In the brief time I've known you, I've never seen you smile quite like you did in your sleep just now."

"You seem so in your element out here," Emily replied, trying to change the subject, and it wasn't hard for Meara to see that, giving her a nod.

"I've always loved the woods," Meara replied. "I spent some time in LA… that was interesting, a hippie commune of sorts…"

"What brought you back here?" Emily questioned.

"My father, he had an accident," Meara replied.

"Is he okay?" she retorted quickly, thinking of her own parents, especially her mom. It was the first time her new friend had mentioned either of her parents.

"He is, he was shot… works for Fish and Game…" Meara responded with a wink and a smile. "He was responding to a call of suspicious gunfire one night, wolf poachers, and he got shot in the exchange."

Emily's heart fluttered. It wasn't the idea of the poachers, more the wolf. She had not thought of real wolves those different from her. Though they crossed her mind, she wondered just how different she was from a real wolf. Were they related or kindred in some way? "But he is okay now?" "Back on the job and everything, but it scared me enough to cause me to come back here, going on a year now." Meara tightened her grip on her legs. "Full moon, a wolf's moon, some may call it, but the only difference is how close it appears to the earth in the sky. But out here where wolves still roam, the moon means something."

"Your father works for Fish and Game?" There was a delay in reaction by Emily. She thought about Don Martin.

Meara smiled. "You met my father already."

Emily gasped. She didn't even know her roommate's last name. Or that she was having inappropriate thoughts about her father. "I didn't know…"

"It's all right. It's a small town," Meara pulled her legs tighter into her meditation position as she stretched her neck up, looking at the cloudless sky. "My dad… he's a good guy. Small town…" She paused, looking around. "There is nothing wrong with that. He deserves to be happy. My mother, she wasn't a saint… I guess I take more after her." There was a long pause between the two of them. "So, there is another reason I wanted you to come with me tonight." Meara had a smile on her face Emily could only describe as mischievous.

Chapter Seven

Emily followed Meara a mile. One after another, through the dark paths and dense trails, barely keeping to anything more noticeable than a deer trail. As the field broke open, she couldn't see any vehicles, but she picked up the scents of a lot of people. She took a deeper breath, and she paused, her heart racing. Before she could speak, Meara was trotting toward the building. She could hear the music, the sound of people having fun. She took in a deeper scent. There were others. Others like her inside. Emily gasped. "Meara," she muttered. The other woman barely broke from her trot to look back.

"I promise, this is worth your time," Emily started moving forward, looking around her as she approached the building.

As she entered the door, there were fifty people there, their scents meshing. It was hard for her to retrieve who was who. More importantly, who was like her. The music was loud, and a man danced around on stage wearing a mask straight out of a horror movie with tentacles falling all around. At a distance, it looked like dreadlocks attached to the mask. He screamed for everyone to dance and jump; it was almost as noticeable after she quit focusing on the mask and his muscular bare chest. He was wearing a kilt and large combat boots. It was then he screamed out to the crowd, and everyone in the club did just as he asked. Emily started to shake, feeling Meara's hand on hers, dragging Emily further into the chaos. Emily had a tough time breathing as she looked around. All she could think about was Lauren's message about others like her in the mid-northwest. She didn't think it would come so easily. That there would be so many like her. She'd get a flash of others, their eyes glowing in the lights every now and again, and she began to panic. Meara still held a tight grip on her wrist as she jumped up and down. She barely knew the young woman, but she was certain her father didn't know about his daughter's nightly conquests. "About once a month, they hold these raves. They usually go all night."

"Has anyone ever…" Emily paused, getting a look at the lead singer's eyes. Even through his horrific mask, she could see the amber glow. He was a wolf as well. "Gone missing after one of these… raves?"

Meara gave her a questioning glare after she stopped dancing.

Emily panicked as she took a long deep breath. "I…" She looked around as she plotted her escape. "I'll be right back."

It only took a few moments to find a bathroom. She splashed water on her face. The scent of the other wolves was stronger now. She took a long deep breath glaring at her reflection. She needed to get Meara out of here. Even though she didn't owe the young woman anything, she needed to get her a safe distance from those like her. The bathroom door opened as three women entered. She knew they were wolves at once. She turned and started to weave past them, but one of them put their hand on her chest, pushing her back against the counter.

"Stay," the blonde said, almost like she was ordering an obedient dog to stay put.

Emily growled as she looked down at the other woman's hand, and a small laugh echoed in her ear.

"Don't," said a tall woman with large afro hair and a noticeable full smile who had taken up a position at the side of the door. She was smiling, looking more at the blonde-haired person who Emily could still feel on her chest. The woman at the door was dressed in jeans and a simple t-shirt.

"We're not going to hurt you," said the second woman. She was skinner and shorter than the other two, with half her head shaved, showing an elaborate dragon tattoo. Her skin was flawless, and she smiled at Emily as she stood at the wall opposite the entrance to the room. Her nose was petite and sharp like the rest of her features.

The third, a busty blonde with pale skin, took a step back, removed her hand from Emily's chest, and then checked each of the stalls to be sure no one else was inside the bathroom before she nodded to the first.

"Of all the clubs in all the world," the first woman said with a thick southern accent as she stepped away from the door.

"You managed to find your way into ours," the third spoke with a growl. The woman's accent was no different from most of the people she had met in Oregon. "Who are you, and what are you doing here? This is pack territory."

"I'm sorry," Emily quickly replied as she tried to gather herself and stand up tall to face the three others. She wondered how she would get out of here if they wanted to attack her.

"I think she's scared," the second woman said, taking a step toward her. "You have nothing to be frightened of, my dear." The woman placed her hand out between them. "I'm Bethany." Her accent was somewhat like the blondes, though there was a distinctly proper way to the way she spoke.

"Julianne," the blonde growled.

"Alma," the first woman said as she approached, holding a handout. As she moved away from the door, it opened, and Meara stepped in.

"There you are," Meara said, looking at Emily. "And I see you've made some new friends."

Emily wadded her hands into fists fighting to keep the wolf in more than ever now. She knew she needed to get out of the bathroom.

"We've met before," Julianne said with a smile turning to face Meara. "You're a local?"

"And you're Liam Bell's daughter." Meara sneered.

Emily took a moment to shift through the women, grabbing Meara by her arm and pulling her along to the door.

"You've protested against my father's company," Julianne said with a big smile.

"Listen," Alma cut in, mostly talking to Emily. "There is an after party." Emily didn't even realize the music had stopped. "You are both invited."

Emily all but dragged Meara from the room. When the door was shut behind them, she turned to look at Meara. "I think I'm ready to go home."

Meara glanced backward and then at Emily. "Don't let those girls scare you. They're harmless. They're wannabe biker chicks. They're all around these parts and, like their brainless companions, are all bluff."

Emily wanted to scream at Meara, tell her how much trouble the other women truly were, and get her as far away from them as she could, but she knew it wouldn't work. The three women exited the bathroom, giving Emily a look as they passed. Alma and Bethany didn't worry her. But the other, Julianne, her scent was familiar. It wasn't from the lake, but she could smell death on the young woman. "I know women like that. Almost all harmless until you back one into a corner and they pull a knife… or worse." Emily thought about how easily one of them could rip through Meara. She had not intended to make a new friend and didn't want to be the reason for her death.

"We can go if you want, but I promise you, there is nothing to worry about," Meara placed her arm in Emily's. Emily let her pull her along.

Emily remained quiet the entire way back to their camp. She wanted to flee, but knowing she couldn't smell the other wolves was comforting. Or hear them. She did her best to use all her senses on the hike back. She couldn't let anything happen to Meara. It would be all her fault.

"What was that back there?" Meara questioned. It was obvious she was angry. Emily could almost see her heating up as she turned to face her once she lit the lantern. "I mean, I've only known you a few days… should I be worried?" The woman crossed her arms against her chest.

Emily wanted to say yes. "About?" She knew the younger woman was referring to her, not the other women at the club.

"You!" She could hear Meara grit her teeth.

"I'm sorry," Emily replied. She was at a loss as to what to say. The truth wasn't a choice.

"You seemed like a cool chick… someone who just needed a little help," Meara said. "But now…" The woman was shaking her head.

Emily sighed. "I don't do well with crowds. I'm sorry."

"Stop apologizing." Meara grimaced. It was like all the air went out of the woman's body. She sat down in her position, crossing her legs and letting her wrist fall on her knees. Emily watched her intently as she took a long deep breath and slowly exhaled. "We all have our quirks." The woman smiled. Meara's demeanor shifted so quickly that Emily didn't know how to take it.

Emily never saw them coming. Never smelled them. And didn't hear them until they were already upon them. There was no time to react. At least five wolves, still in their human forms. She recognized at least one of their scents as Julianne Bell. Emily was on her stomach and could only see blackness. A bag had been quickly put over her head, and her body flung to the ground in front of them. It knocked the wind out of her, and she felt rough hands on the back of her neck, followed by a growl. Then the screams. Meara started screaming and never stopped. She'd been looking in the other direction when they came out of the darkness. She screamed until there was no more air left in her lungs and then started again. It was followed by a dull thud and silence, only the breathing of the other wolves.

"What now?" a male voice questioned. It was obvious that it was a man also holding her in place, so at least two of the other wolves were male.

"We take her with us," Julianne said.

"She's not like us," the man replied.

Only a growl followed as a reply. Emily tried to speak, but she found she was still breathless. The man on her back kept her pinned to the ground. "Ms. Meyer has a lot of questions to answer."

Emily shuttered at the mention of her sir's name. She tried to struggle.

"Stay still. We're not going to harm you," the man who kept her pinned to the ground spoke up.

"That's not for us to decide," Julianne replied. She could tell the other woman was still growling.

Emily felt a prick on her arm, and the feeling of herself starting to doze off was almost immediate. "I promise you, nothing is going to happen to…."

Emily woke suddenly.

"Meara…" she muttered as she tried to clear her eyes. Everything was foggy, and she couldn't quite tell where she was.

"They gave you some sort of tranquilizer." It was Meara.

Emily turned, looking back into a corner. It was a van of some sort. "Where are we?"

"Are they serial killers… I don't…" Meara started to say. "I don't understand."

Emily did. "I'm sorry."

"You… you know these people?" Meara questioned. "The way you acted with those in the bathroom…"

"No," she quickly replied. "I know people like them."

"They're awake!" Emily heard a male voice call out from the outside of the van. She could smell them now. The man was the one who had her pinned to the ground.

Emily put her hand back between her and Meara as the door opened. There were three of them. Emily didn't recognize any of them; only the man standing closest to the door was a familiar scent. The one who pinned her. "Why are we here?" Emily quickly questioned. "You can let Meara go… she knows nothing about you… me…" Emily was stuttering. She didn't quite know how to explain it without letting her young friend know just how much danger she was in.

"I'm not going anywhere without you," Meara quickly piped in.

"You can come with us," the woman said. It was then she got a better look at her and recognized her half-shaved head. Her senses were dulled, and she didn't recognize Bethany's scent.

"Nothing is going to happen to you or your friend," the other man said. He was older as well, in his fifties or sixties, and he was smiling. With a full gray beard and thinning hair, something about his smile made her trust this man, even though she knew she shouldn't. She sensed no aggression toward her from either of these two. She felt Meara's hand on hers as they followed them out of the van and down a graveled road.

"Where are we?" Meara questioned.

"Some place someone one like you shouldn't be." A bald man stepped out of nowhere. Emily was having problems picking up scents. She tried to use all her other senses. The tranquilizer was messing with them. "We have questions for your friend." The man growled, and Emily could feel the man's eyes travel all over her.

"Did he just growl at you?" Meara questioned, squeezing up close to her.

"She doesn't know," Emily quickly said.

"It's too late for that." Julianne appeared. She was also growling.

Emily stopped in her tracks, pulling Meara close to her back. "What is this?"

The older man sighed. "Miss Emily Meyer, I'm Harrison," he said, holding out his hand.

"She's an outsider," a large man said, also appearing from the direction of the bald man. Emily's senses were coming back to her now. She could smell distinct smells and hear others in the bushes, it was not yet daylight, but she could pick out a dozen or more scents of other wolves in the woods around her.

Another appeared. This one was large and half wolf. She heard Meara lose her breath and her heart race. Meara tried to pull away. Emily turned to grab the younger woman by her cheeks.

"Look at me," Emily sternly spoke. Meara's eyes shifted to her for a moment and then tried to find the wolf. She could see her throat; the woman was beginning to panic. She could tell her heart rate was all over the place. Her eyes were wide with fear. "Meara, look at me." Again, Meara shifted her eyes to investigate Emily's. "I will not let them hurt you."

"What the fuck...?" she mumbled.

"Close your eyes," Emily said, but it was obvious her friend wasn't going to. "Meara."

Meara again looked into her eyes. "My nightmare." Emily wanted to cry. This was her nightmare, and she had brought someone else into it now. Meara's lips parted to speak, but nothing came out. "It's real… the girls back at the club…"

Meara's already pale complexion was ghostly.

"I'm sorry…" Emily turned, looking into Meara's eyes. "Nothing is going to happen to you… I promise."

"Not a promise you can make," the large man said.

"Madison," Bethany said harshly. "Quiet."

"We know about West Virginia, Devon, Lauren." Harrison now walked closer. "I had missed you by only a day, and I tracked you until I lost you… then I got the call from Sheriff Banks." Emily remembered the call while she was at the sheriff's department. The question was whether she was one of theirs or not. It all made more sense now.

"The sheriff… he knows…" Emily was shocked. She held Meara close to her and tried to keep an eye on the other wolves she considered a threat.

"Sheriff Banks has known about us for a long time," Harrison replied. "He tries to keep the peace as long as we keep our true selves hidden from the rest of the community."

"Why did you bring us here?" Emily quickly questioned.

Meara pulled away from Emily as more emerged from the surrounding wilderness. Emily knew there was nothing she could do if so many of them had wanted to attack her or Meara. "I don't understand," Meara said. Her voice quivered with terror.

Emily followed her new friend's footsteps, trying to keep herself between Meara and all the other wolves.

"Where are you going, little girl?" Emily turned to look at the large man they called Madison. "I don't think we've been introduced." The man's lips trembled, exposing his enlarged canines.

"Back off," Emily growled, quickly putting her body between Meara and the large man. But she could feel the heat coming off him, making her uncomfortable as she looked into his soft brown eyes.

"We have gone about this all wrong," Bethany spoke up. "We are not hostile. You and your friend can go as you please."

Emily heard at least two distinct growls coming from the pack of wolves.

"We wanted you to know there are others like you here," Harrison said. "Looking to live among people. We mean them no more of a threat than we do you."

"Yeah, you seem friendly," Meara piped in sarcastically.

"Exposing us to your friend was a mistake in youth." Emily saw several of them glare in Julianne's direction. Though the blonde seemed younger than everyone else apart from Meara, she had some sort of privilege among them. "Only you were supposed to have been brought."

"We trust the daughter of Don Martin will keep our secret as well," Harrison said as Emily looked at Meara, who was shocked by the revelation her father knew about the werewolves as well.

"Who in this town doesn't know about our existence?" Emily quickly questioned.

"Only a small handful know about us. Several of our pack call Oakridge home," Bethany said.

"My father?" Meara questioned.

"The wolf your father was shot protecting was one of us… though he doesn't know this," the older woman replied.

"Is that why one of them was killed?" Emily knew she shouldn't have said anything but the more she thought about it the situation, having Meara surrounded, she kept flashing back to the body in the lake.

Whispers and gasps took over the group as each seemed to question what Emily was saying. Even looking at each other with some level of distrust.

"A body was found in the lake… shredded, killed by a wolf," Emily growled. She could tell by the reactions no one knew, but she wanted to continue to prod. It would make it better for her and Meara to leave. "And I can smell the killer on her." She pointed at Julianne. She kept pointing at the young wolf as everyone else looked at her with no surprise.

Julianne growled, "*Liar!*"

"It's an internal matter," Bethany said, attempting to turn away. It was obvious the woman was angry. They knew who the killer was. "We're sorry for how we made our introductions. We just wanted you to know you were not alone."

"A pretty risky way of doing it," Emily replied.

"Not really," the bald skinny man growled.

"She'll keep our secret just like her father or…"

"Julianne, *enough*," Harrison suddenly stopped her from finishing her threat. "Morgan will take you back to town. We are terribly sorry for all of this."

Morgan was the first man she had seen. He had short brown hair and a scruffy beard neatly trimmed to his face. He crossed over to them and opened the van back up for them to enter. Once she realized he was wearing a kilt, she knew him as the singer.

"Told you everything was going to be all right." Emily turned, looking back at the others, but as quickly as so many other wolves had appeared, they were now gone.

Not a lot was said until they were back at Meara's house and Morgan was gone. The other woman had regained her color, and no longer seemed as nervous or terrified. The moment the door was closed behind them, she spoke, "What the ever-loving fuck just happened...?" She could see the pulse in her throat begin to race again.

Emily remained by the door; she didn't know what to say. "Werewolves are real... and you... my new roommate..."

Emily replied with just a nod of her head. She was afraid of looking the other woman in the eye. She thought she had found a safe place.

"You're a werewolf?"

"Yes..." is all Emily could bring herself to reply.

"How... when..." Meara turned, going to the kitchen and getting two beers from the fridge. The sun was just beginning to peek through the door and curtains at her back, filtering into the otherwise dark room. "Fuck," Meara muttered softly, returning to the room with both. She sat across the table. "And my father..."

"I didn't know about your father…" Emily crossed the room, standing at the edge of the table. "Do you want me to leave?"

"Hell no," Meara quickly replied. "With what I just… this why you are on the run? And why you were able to do what you did to that dickhead back at the diner." Meara took a drink from her beer. "And my father knew…" Meara returned to finish her earlier thought. "How the hell…?"

"Huh?" Emily responded, trying to keep track of what Meara was asking. "We don't know that your father knows about us. Just that he was shot protecting a were—it's possible he doesn't know."

"How did it happen to you?" Meara questioned.

Emily recanted her story. From Devon to Colin and Lauren and how she had told her to go northwest. That there were others. Packs.

"I didn't think I'd find one so easily, not sure I even wanted to… I just wanted to get someplace…" Emily looked at the beer in front of her, grabbing it and downing more than half in one swallow.

"Safe?" Meara interrupted.

"Oakridge no longer seems like it is a safe place…" Emily said before she finished off her beer.

"I don't know what to do," Emily responded. It had become a common part of her life. Being lost.

"You stay… until we get something figured out."

Chapter Eight

⚜ ——————————— ⚜

For two days, Emily had remained in her room entirely except to go to the bathroom and the kitchen. In that time, she hadn't even seen or heard Meara, but for the most part, the other woman's scent wasn't as prevalent. Emily had even postponed her date with Don over text, and she hadn't spoken to him much since. Part of her wondered if she had ruined her chance with him, but at the same time, she wasn't sure what she wanted to be anything there with the man. She couldn't help but wonder just how much about her kind Don knew.

Emily pulled into the diner's parking spaces. She had picked up an extra shift, taking one of Meara's who had called in sick. Emily sat there, looking at the people going in and out, most not knowing the threat they lived among. She could easily leave, go someplace else. But Meara was right. She needed someplace to figure things out, even if it was only temporary. She could learn more about the other part of it. How to control the wolf. She smiled at the thought. If she had control of the wolf, she could return home. To Ashley. To her mother. To pay her last respects to Colin.

The two-black SUVs pulled in beside her, breaking her from her daydream. She watched as six men exited the vehicles, three from each. The smell hit her; though the window was barely cracked, she knew at once. It was him. She watched the five men, all in their nice business suits, strange attire for the small town. She was sure it was the first time she had seen anyone in a true, elegantly pressed suit since she had gotten here. She could see their lips moving but couldn't hear what they were saying. It was only a moment before all but one left, the others disappearing into the clerk's office right next door to Rosie's. He drew in a long drag off his cigarette as he looked at her, their eyes locked on one another, sending a chill all over her body. He glanced to the ground, tossing and mushing it out, careful not to scuff his shined shoes. He unbuttoned his jacket and walked toward the truck, inspecting the old beat-up Chevy. He stopped at the window, still looking over the truck. Emily looked forward toward Rosie's. Too much thinking, and now she was paying for it. She slowly rolled the window down, and the moment it was clear, he crossed his arms on the door frame looking inside, not at Emily, but at her surroundings.

"Liam Bell," he pronounced.

Emily continued to give him a questioning look as he reached out to shake her hand when it was obvious she wasn't going to. He retreated his pleasantries and stepped back from the truck.

"I do not believe I've had the pleasure, but I followed your scent a week ago now. You're new here." He placed his hands carefully inside his jacket pockets. "You are new to these parts." Emily continued to stare without answers. Liam took in a deep breath, closing his eyes and enjoying the moment. He smiled as he opened his dark eyes, giving a glance at the clerk's office before stepping back into the truck. "It's impolite not to give me your name."

"Sarah."

"It is nice to meet you, Sarah." He grinned.

"You killed a man," she said loud enough if there had been anyone close could have heard.

Liam only smiled. His smile made Emily angry. There was a confidence there. "The pack takes what it needs." Emily tilted her head. "Ah, naive little girl, you're not part of a pack? What happened to the one who gifted you?" The man gave off a much different attitude and persona than any of the wolves she had met from the pack. This man considered himself something better than even them. She didn't need to really know anymore.

"I ripped his throat out." She grinned, trying to make herself seem threatening, but he only grinned.

"Child, there is a whole entire world out here you have yet to discover." He turned away from the truck, hearing the others exit the clerk's office. He continued to give her a big smile looking back. Emily watched as they left before she started her own truck and pulled away.

Emily made her way back to the lake. She found a place where she could easily get the truck off the road, and it would still be hard for anyone to see her unless they were looking. She walked knee-high out into the water, taking in a cool breath of the cold air. She wanted to scream. Liam Bell reminded her not of Devon, the man responsible for the nightmare she found herself in, but her own father. The arrogance. The fact that he was never wrong whether he was or not. They were the same in personality.

The phone in her back pocket began to buzz. Louder and louder, she'd forgotten completely about the phone. No one had the number except Meara. But she quickly recognized the 304. Emily didn't recognize anything but the area code going with the number. She sighed. This could not be a miss dialed call. She clicked answer and slowly lifted the phone to her ear.

"Hello?" Emily heard silence for a moment and then a heavy sigh. She thought she was going to break down at that moment. "Mom?" Emily bit down hard on her lower lip. Was this a dream? A very cruel dream?

"She is having a rough go at it," the voice on the other end of the line was unmistakable. No matter how long it had been since she heard her best friend's voice.

"Ashley!" Emily muttered.

"You should consider calling your mother," Ashley responded. There was a considerable coldness to her familiar voice. No matter how long it had been since she'd spoken to her best friend, she would never forget her voice. "She has taken your disappearance hard, and it's taken a toll on your parents' marriage… Not that they had the best marriage to begin with. Your father is a pompous ass." Silence remained for what felt like several minutes. "I miss your face."

"I miss you so much." Emily wiped tears from her face. She felt like her knees were going to buckle under as she tried to control her panicked breathing.

"You can come home, you know… I'll help you through this," Ashley responded.

"I can't." Emily wanted to scream for so many reasons. She didn't realize how much she had missed her friend. "How did you…"

"Get this number?" Ashley cut her off. "I was contacted online by a woman named Meara, and she gave it to me, said you could use a friend. She found me through social media site where I had a missing person page dedicated to you…"

"You what?" Emily questioned as she gritted her teeth. Ashley might not have known her specific location, but she was familiar enough with what she was going through to know she was missing for a reason.

"It kept your mother feeling less hopeless that someone was trying to do something. I had to do it to help her… you should call, Emily," Ashley responded. "And Meara is a friend… "

"What else did she tell you?" Emily quickly questioned.

"Nothing… I'm assuming she knows about you?" Ashley said.

"She does… she and I… I've run across a pack of people like me, and I don't know what to do," Emily said.

"What are they like… are they like Devon?" Ashley quickly questioned.

"One… I don't know. He reminds me of my father's arrogance," Emily said. She could easily make the connection between Liam Bell and her father in the way they carried themselves.

"So, an intelligent psychopath," Ashley responded. "An egomaniac who will never admit to being wrong."

Emily wanted for just a moment to ask how her father was, but the feeling quickly left her. She would contact her mother. "The others, I don't know… They didn't present themselves in the friendliest of ways."

"I've known you most of my life… I've never known you to let fear rule you." Ashley responded. "You were a star athlete. You played against boys on the lacrosse teams. I've never known you to back away from a fight. Not even from your father."

Emily wanted to say, *look where that got me.*

"You learn from them, you get stronger, and you get control, and you come home. For me. For your mother. To get your life back. You are stronger than the wolf," Ashley responded. "You come home because we love you."

"I don't think I am," Emily replied.

"Don't be whiny bitch. That's not you," Ashley snapped in a harsh tone.

Emily was crying harder now, trying to keep Ashley from knowing.

"You will beat this," Ashley said. "Because it is who you are. You just will, and I have faith in you."

Emily turned, hearing a car door slam. "Ashley, I have to go. There is someone here."

"Call me back," Ashley responded.

"I love you," Emily smiled, a little more confident. Ashley always had that effect on her.

"I love you, too."

Emily hung up, placing the phone back in her pocket. "Isn't the water freezing?" The young deputy stopped up to the edge of the bank. "Sarah Jenkins, right?"

"It's not that bad," Emily responded. "I don't think we've met officially." It was the same deputy who was with the sheriff the day at the church.

"Kaylan Patrick," he said, looking around at the lake. "You alone?"

The man made her uncomfortable. "My friend's down the beach a way…"

"Meara? I don't think you've had time to really make any other friends in the community," Kaylan quickly responded. There was an arrogance in his voice. Kaylan rested his hand on his hips, the right hand tapping on the handle of his pistol.

"Can I help you, Officer?"

"I'm curious about a stranger in my community who assaults our citizens, is all." He smirked, still tapping on the handle of the gun.

"Maybe your citizens shouldn't beat the hell out of waitresses," Emily jabbed. If she were close enough, she would have smacked the officer. She could hear him grumble, even at their distance.

"Keep your head down, Miss Jenkins. I wouldn't want anything to happen to your pretty face." Kaylan continued to tap his pistol only faster as he turned away.

Emily sighed. She wanted to say something more, keep the man close so she could get to the beach and confront him. But he was another threat to add to her list, wife beating rednecks, their police officer friends, and a werewolf with a god complex.

Emily wanted to talk to Meara. She wasn't angry about her new friend having contacted Ashley, but she wanted to know more, especially since she had been avoiding her for days. She didn't expect to find Don Martin sitting in the drive when she pulled in.

"Have you seen Meara?" he questioned as Emily exited the truck.

"Not since this morning," Emily responded. Emily had not seen her that morning but knew she was safely in her room when she left for work.

"I needed to check in on you as well. Be careful when you are out around the lake or in the woods." Don was paler than the last time she'd seen him. His beard had been trimmed, but there was grayer there now than before.

"Why?" She knew why but needed him to say it. She wasn't certain he knew about the wolves, but she was almost certain he still didn't know she was one, and she wanted to keep it that way for as long as she could. Or if he did… she should tell him. She was torn, not knowing what she should do.

"Another body has been found," he replied. "This time, not a bear. So just be careful when you're out, for me." Don stepped away. "So, about that raincheck?" Part of her had hoped he wouldn't bring it up so soon. "How does tomorrow night sound?"

"Yes, call it seven," she replied. She had surprised herself with how quickly she answered. He waved before he climbed back into his jeep and pulled away. Emily saw the other man, barely noticeable in the shadows of the woods. The Black man stepped out into the light when he was sure the ranger was gone. She could smell him. The closer he walked, she knew she was face to face with another of the pack.

"Don Martin is a good man," he said with a big grin.

"Liam sent you?" It seemed like at every turn, people were sneaking up on her today.

"Obviously." The man ran his hand through the scruffy dark beard. "He wanted me to deliver you a message. And invite, tonight out on Robinson Road. Your friend Meara knows where. Come with her."

"And if I refuse?"

"I wouldn't." He turned his back walking down the drive, and paused. "The man they found, it was an accident, come tonight… and I wouldn't leave town. I am sure Liam would consider it an insult, and he may find someone to take his hurt feelings out on." Emily knew the man meant Meara.

Emily stood staring at all her clothing lying on the bed. So little to choose from, and she couldn't help but think she was doing something stupid by agreeing to come along. She heard the door to the home open and then quickly shut. "Meara." She rushed to the door.

Meara was just sitting the keys on the counter as she turned. "Hey," the woman smiled. She looked ghostly. Her skin was pale and her eyes dark. She'd not been sleeping.

"Are you okay?" Emily quickly questioned.

"I am…" Meara turned away, walking to the fridge, sitting something inside. "So, I hear we have some sort of get-together to go to tonight," Meara said. She pulled a revolver from the back of her pants and set it on the counter.

Emily took a step backward.

"It's not for you," Meara replied. "One of the advantages of living in a rural area… guns are easy to access. Same goes for specialized ammo. I'm not sure if silver will do anything, but a few days ago, I thought werewolves were just something from horror movies or sexy tween flicks."

Emily wanted to smile. "You don't have to go."

"Oh, I'm going," Meara quickly replied. "The question is, what are we going to wear?"

The drive there was a short one. As they turned off onto a side road, Emily had to ask. "How many people are going to be there?"

"Twenty, maybe about that," Meara replied. The woman had smiled off, and, on the trip, she knew there was some curiosity there. Meara wanted to know more.

There was a series of about fifteen vehicles lined up, and she pulled in beside the last. She could see people in the middle of the field all sitting, standing around a huge bonfire. She could tell as the wind shifted there were several wolves, but most of them were humans. Was Liam Bell setting her up? She looked up toward the sky. It would be dark in a few hours. "What is this?"

"Liam Bell throws a big bonfire every time he returns, inviting some people from around town. He does it to show he is part of the town, but now I realize it was for something much different…" Meara replied. "It usually coincides with something else that keeps most of the God-fearing populace occupied elsewhere while we deviants have some fun." Meara was in her state here. Her eyes lit up as they approached the bonfires. She was showing no fear now.

Emily smiled. "Why not invite the entire town then? Why just a few select people?"

As they got closer to the group, Emily quickly noticed a woman with large pink dreadlocks and a nose ring. She was wearing only a bra and jeans as she danced around the fire.

Emily could smell the strong scent of marijuana as they got closer.

"That's Bailey… I'll have to introduce you," Meara said with a smile. Emily recognized the name as the voice on the other end of Don Martin's radio. They walked through the group, and Emily kept an eye out on everyone around. She could smell the other wolves but could not pick them out of the crowd. There were too many scents mixing with the smoke.

"I am glad to see you decided to join us, ladies." Emily took a step back as he came from behind them. "I did not have the chance to introduce myself earlier, Chamberlain." He took Emily by the hand and kissed it before releasing her. Then he kissed Meara's. Emily looked to her new friend and then back to the guy. His eyes glowed yellow, and he smiled. He was dressed in a dark suit with a scarf. He looked out of place. "Come with me." Meara held a tight grip on her arm. "Meara can come as well. She's now part of this world."

Emily slipped away with him. Emily waited until they were far enough away before speaking. "How many?"

"Here or in the pack?" Chamberlain smiled. "Seven here tonight, the actually numbers in the pack I'm not certain of…I've mostly played as Liam's bodyguard, and he is waiting for you."

They walked a good deal away from the others, Liam was not alone, and Emily knew at once the third man was also a wolf. "I'm here."

"I see that," Liam said, lifting his beer into the air.

"You didn't have to threaten me," Emily replied. Meara's grip was tight on her arm.

"Oh, I believe I did, Emily Meyer," she took two quick steps backward right into Chamberlain. "Quite the mess you left behind in West Virginia, and here you were criticizing me for one death."

"I never… I didn't kill all of them," Emily quickly replied. "How did you?"

"It is our business," the third man spoke, he was bigger than the other two, taller and more muscular, and she could smell the wolf pheromones coming off him. He was more wolf than human, his short dark hair and beard to match. She recognized him from the other night. "Whenever there are deaths in the news, wild animal attacks we notice, we watch to see if it is one of us. How many did you leave dead in your wake?" Emily wanted to growl. She instantly did not like this third man.

"I told you. I didn't kill them," Emily said.

"Who then?" Chamberlain questioned.

"Two others…"

"And they are dead now," Liam said. He knew. It was written all over his face. "Why are you here, Ms. Meyer?" Emily did not want to correct him about Lauren.

"You came northwest from your home. The Midwest, all the way to the ocean, is a hotbed for wolves," she turned to see another man and woman walking toward them. The other two wolves. She crossed her arms against her chest and eyed each. She picked up on both of their scents before they even got to her, Morgan, and Alma.

"I'd like to introduce you to Madison." Chamberlain pointed to the big man who was already with them, the one she didn't like.

"We've met." Emily fought back a snarl, thinking about how Madison had been so hostile toward them a few nights before.

"Morgan." The fourth man, with his long hair and mischievous smile, was the least of her worries. He was a short man, shorter than her, he wore no shirt, and it showed a muscular upper body. Mostly she smelled alcohol more than the wolf on him. "And last, but certainly not least, Alma Renee, you've met." It was the way he said Alma's name, a hint of trying to talk down to the woman as if she were a child, using her middle name.

"What do you want with me?" Emily questioned.

Liam took a big drink as he faced her. "We want to invite you to join the pack."

Emily looked at each. "Why the hell would I do that?"

"This life isn't an easy one to go at it alone." She turned to see Alma was now the closest one to her. With her distinctive tan eyes, she smiled. Her skin was flawless.

"You've already killed one person." She looked around. At least two of them, Alma and Morgan, showed a little shock at what she was saying.

"What is she talking about?" Morgan questioned. Liam wiped his lips, turning away. "Liam?"

"Wrong place at the wrong time," Chamberlain said.

"We don't kill," Alma quickly added. Emily backed out of the center of the group. Alma was close to Chamberlain with a stern look on her face. Morgan watched Liam.

"I am the alpha," Liam turned to look back at the others. Both Morgan and Alma took a step back. It was obvious. There was fear there. "I make the decisions, and this is my pack."

"No." Emily watched Alma take a deep breath taking two quick steps toward Liam. There was an intense fierceness radiating off the woman, and everyone was now paying attention to her as she spoke. "You're not the only leader in this pack." By now, Emily was several steps away from the group and watched as the smallest of them took two more quick steps toward Liam. It happened in a flash. Madison hit her with a backhand slap. The largest of the group had moved with a speed she never thought possible. She watched Liam with his big smile as he leaned down with an outreached hand. Alma took it, and he helped her up. The entire time the small woman watched, Madison and Emily could hear why. The man was growling and breathing heavily, the sun was still out, but he was on the edge of transformation.

"Do not question me," Liam said with a smile. Alma backed away into Morgan, who had not moved. Neither had Chamberlain.

"We have an agreement within the pack. No human casualties," Morgan spoke up.

"Wrong place, wrong time," Chamberlain said, repeating himself. It was obvious that he and Madison were along with Liam, but the other two, they still had their humanity. Emily turned, looking back at the group around the fire, but no one had noticed, and she could not help but wonder. There were others from the pack in town. Where were they? Alma looked back at her. Her eyes were yellow. She could see as she gritted her teeth that she was on the edge of a transformation.

"We are giving Ms. Meyer the wrong impression, yet again." She turned back. Liam had closed the distance between them.

"If I refuse to be a part of your pack?" Emily questioned.

"It is your decision and not one to be made in the heat of the moment but to mull over, to come to your decision," Liam said. "No one here will harm you; I can promise you."

"And the people close to me?"

"None of these people are close to you," Liam smiled as he turned, walking away from her. "You're new to town, and you barely know them, but for the time being, I promise there will be no harm." She could see the deceiving look in his eyes.

Emily turned, walking away from them, practically dragging Meara along with her, giving the wolves a glance back along the path. There was no stopping her. She only wished to leave.

Emily sat with her head on the steering wheel. It was just starting to grow dark when she pulled into the drive. Meara sat beside her, having said hardly a word since they left. What was she going to do? Could she run? She did not owe the people of the town anything—she could run. Go southwest, still moving away from her family and away from the pack. They had said most of the Northwest was werewolf territory, was that why she was drawn to the area? The small town of Oakridge was the first place she came to that she felt she could hide in plain sight, even if it was for a few days.

Emily entered her home and at once knew something wasn't right. She could smell it, feel it. The cold air rushed in from a back door.

"Hello?"

She knew there had been another wolf in her home. She tossed her keys down onto the table inside the door and crossed the living room. There were two doors, always locked. The first one she came across was wide open, and as she passed through, so was the second leading out into the night air.

"Son of a bitch." She stepped out into the light. She was glad she came in while Meara was still in the vehicle.

"He promised to leave me alone!" she yelled out. Her head held high in the air, and she took in a deep breath. She watched the wilderness. She knew she was close to the lake; it would have been easy for a wolf to track her back to her home and from the lake. She stepped back into her home, securing both doors as she stepped through. Her wolf wanted out. She wanted to hunt the other down, get answers and exact some sort of revenge for the breaking in of her newfound sanctuary. Meara was coming in through the front door as she sighed.

"Are you going to leave?" Meara questioned. She could see a growing sadness in the other woman's expression.

"I don't know," Emily replied.

Chapter Nine

Emily had gone to work the next morning with a lot on her mind. She knew she had a date that evening and wanted to get through the day. Every time the bell on the door to the diner dinged, she looked to see who was coming in. Once, she thought she saw a fully transformed werewolf coming in and sitting down at the counter to order coffee. Emily sat down at one of the booths during her break with a plate of bacon and eggs with toast. She had started to dig through them with her fork when Allison took a seat across from her. She watched the woman take off her glasses and at once saw her bruised eye.

"What the hell…?"

"Don't worry," Allison said. Emily watched the woman dig into her gravy and biscuits with chopped sausage.

"Where is he?" she questioned quickly, now ignoring her own plate.

"I called the police on him," she replied. Emily couldn't help but think about Kaylan Patrick. "We won't have to worry about him anymore."

"We?"

Allison picked at her food. "I have a daughter… it's not his," she replied.

"Where is she now?" Emily questioned.

"With her father," Allison replied with a frown. "Robert was a good man… he and I didn't match well. He is a wonderful father." Emily also frowned. She wondered how the meek woman in front of her ended up with someone like Eugene. "Does your head hurt?"

"I'm all right," Emily replied.

"I…" The other woman was older than Emily. She stuttered as she spoke, looking out the window. "I wanted to thank you for coming to my defense the other night. You didn't have to do that."

"I did," Emily replied.

"You didn't," she answered. "That is why I wanted to thank you. Most people wouldn't put themselves in harm's way like you did."

"Make me a promise you'll stay away from him," Emily replied.

Emily came home, placed groceries for her dinner in the fridge, and quickly went to her room to get dressed. She looked at her bags. She hadn't even hung her clothing back up from the day before.

"Stuff may not fit you the way you'd like, but I have some stuff for your date if you're interested." Meara leaned in the door.

"I'm fine," Emily lied. She had already decided on going simple for the date, "Is this weird?"

"What, that you're going out on a date with my father?" Meara questioned.

Emily nodded as a reply.

"Yeah, as is the fact that you're a werewolf… I'm a pretty free-thinking girl, Emily… or Sarah… which do you prefer me to call you?" Meara questioned.

"Sarah… for now," Emily replied.

"I only ask that you don't hurt him… he has been through a lot," Meara replied. She started to exit the room and stopped with a big smile. "Yeah, it's a little weird, and plus, there is the whole he knows about what you are…" There was a hint of laughter in her voice as she left the room.

Emily smiled as she pulled the dark knee-length skirt from her bag and a simple loose-fitting dark top.

The knock at the door came early. She hesitated as she crossed to the front door. She was not surprised to see Don on the other side. "Sorry, I know I'm a little early," Don said. "Are you ready?"

Emily stepped out the door. "Yeah, I'm ready."

Emily followed him to the truck, where he opened the passenger door. "My lady." Emily smiled as she stepped inside.

"Thank you."

Emily watched as he circled around the front of the truck. He moved swiftly to the side. "There's not a lot of fancy restaurants to choose from, hope you like steak." It was a short drive to the local steak house, right on the edge of Oakridge. There were many more people inside than Emily expected when they got in. It wasn't long until they were seated and even ordered.

"So, what has brought you to Oregon?" Don questioned after sitting his drink down. Emily looked at the hurricane margarita in front of her.

"I was looking for a fresh start," Emily replied, placing a soda in front of them both.

"So, you're running from something?" He smiled.

Yes, myself, Emily wanted to say as she took a drink, trying to ignore his handsome smile. "I needed a fresh start, and this seemed like a good place for that," Emily replied.

Don smirked.

Emily took a deep breath, and her heart almost stopped. She could smell other wolves, and she nervously looked around the restaurant. It wasn't hard to see them. Liam and Julianne Bell. She couldn't help but stare, to the point she realized Don had noticed her.

"Have you met the Bells?" Don questioned.

"Only in passing," Emily quickly replied before taking another drink.

"He is a nice guy… gives a lot back to the community, more than is actually asked of him," Don replied.

"So, you like the guy?" Emily replied.

"I've never had any problems with him," Don replied.

"He seems like an arrogant asshole," Emily snapped.

"My daughter has a much similar opinion of him," Don replied.

Emily smiled. "Meara."

"This is weird, isn't it?" Don questioned. "I mean, Meara is twenty-two… you're…"

"Twenty-six… yeah, this is a little weird," Emily replied with a smile. "But I'm guessing a charming, handsome guy like you in his mid…"

"I was sixteen when her mom and I had Meara," he quickly replied with a smile.

"So, you're not that much older than me," Emily said. She knew she had other issues standing in the way of her being in a relationship, but she was also lonely. It had been a while since she had been touched by someone who cared, and she couldn't help but realize Don was a nice guy. Or she should take up the offer of Bell, be part of a pack. She would have no reason from there to be lonely. She would be with others like her.

"So, it's not that weird," Don quickly responded.

"It didn't seem to bother Meara," Emily replied.

"Like her mother, she is a handful of trouble and causing me to go gray fast."

"How long have you and her mother been separated," Emily questioned.

"We separated when she was seven… I'm guessing it was the seven-year itch. I really don't know." Don took a long drink.

"You or her?" Emily asked.

"Which of us got the itch?" he smiled. "I'm guessing we both did, she cheated, and I didn't care anymore, really. We tried to make it another year before we got divorced." He took a drink of his wine. "So, any crazy exes in your past I should worry about?"

"None that you need to worry about," she replied with a smile.

"So, you've never been in any serious relationships?" he questioned.

"Never married if that is what you're asking." Emily smiled.

"Ah, so you don't want to talk about it," he replied.

Emily took another drink as the waitress sat the food down for them. "There are no exes you need to worry about. I've had a couple serious ones, but all of those are in the past now."

"So, tell me about Sarah."

"I'm an average girl, I guess," she lied.

"Who enjoys running." She smiled when he said it.

"Yeah, I enjoy running…" Emily paused. She had to know. "I heard someone say they found another body out where the bear was found…" Don's mood instantly changed as he looked away.

"Yeah, but it's not something I believe we need to talk about." He smiled as he looked at her. "Not on a first date, anyways."

"So, this is a date," Emily returned with a smile as she sat up.

"A terrible one, though. Let's see, we've talked about our exes, and now we're talking about death," he replied with a smile.

"It is kind of morbid, isn't it?" She sat her glass down. "So, what would make this better?"

"I'm terrible on dates," Don said, taking a drink.

"Officer Martin, how are you?" The two of them looked at the man at the table. Liam Bell was standing there in his freshly pressed suit, whitened teeth, and salon-styled hair.

"I'm good. How are you, Mr. Bell?" Don replied, standing. The two of them shook hands, and Emily wanted to disappear, not to let the other wolf talk to her at all.

"I'm good. I'm back home for a few weeks before I'm pulled away again. It is good to be home," Liam said as he turned away, looking straight at Emily. She wanted to disappear. "And you, Miss Jenkins, how are you enjoying our quaint little slice of America?"

"Like everywhere else, you take the good with the bad." Emily held back her growl.

"I'd love to give you a tour of my logging facilities sometime. Later this month, I will be having a get-together. You're invited." He had a large smile on his face. "And, of course, you are invited as well."

"Well, thank you, Mr. Bell," Don said.

"I'm not sure how long I'm going to be in town," Emily snipped, and it caused his lips to twitch, but only for a moment before the smile was back.

"Well, if you do, you're more than welcome to come by... so is that friend of yours." He smiled and nodded as he turned, walking away.

"You really don't like him," Don said. "You take after my daughter, I think. Despite what she may tell you, he really isn't that bad. Does a lot around these parts?"

"There is an arrogance about him that I really don't like," Emily said as she continued to watch him. They continued through dinner. It wasn't long until they were both done eating and on their way back.

"You want to come in for a drink?" Emily questioned as they stood at the front door. "Meara still isn't home. We could build a fire out back and get to know each other a little better."

They were in the backyard with a small fire in the fire pit; Emily was lost in her gaze at the flames. "You're really not like other women I've known." Emily wanted to laugh. She was more like others he knew than he thought. But she still wanted to keep that part of her to herself.

As she turned back, Don had closed the distance, and she could feel the heat radiating off him. He leaned in; she didn't think as she kissed him. His lips were chapped, and his breath still tasted of wine from dinner. She felt his hand on her face, it was cold and rough, and she still enjoyed it. It had been too long since she felt the touch of another human. She pulled away, looking at his dull blue eyes.

"What kind of girl do you think I am?" He leaned away with a sly smile.

"I'm sorry," he replied.

She stood circling around, straddling him in his chair and kissed him again quickly.

"I was joking, silly." She smiled.

She could feel his muscular hands on her hips, and excitement ran up her back, goose pimples raised on her arms and neck, and she kissed him again, paying closer attention to his chapped lips. She leaned back, sitting on his upper thighs, and she smiled, gazing into his eyes. She was more than excited. She wanted to rip his clothes off and have him right there by the fire as the snow drifted down on them. She felt a name on her lips, but it wasn't Don's she wanted to whisper but her friend's, someone she was responsible for dying, Colin.

She felt his hands drift up to bare skin on her waist and dropped her head back as she bit down on her own lower lip.

"Okay," she muttered. The excitement was doing more than she thought; she could feel her stomach growl until she caught it in her throat, stopping it from escaping. She knew her eyes had changed as she looked up at the bright moon.

"I can stop if you want," she heard him say as he kissed her neck.

"It's the first date and all. I can't let it go any further." She took a couple of deep breaths as she lowered her head, looked him into his eyes, and gave him a short, soft peck on his lips. "Give you something to look forward to," she felt him kiss her on the forehead before she stood.

"I guess this means there is going to be a second date." He smiled.

Emily only smiled.

Chapter Ten

"Boy, that was close, wasn't it?" Emily darted up from her sleep. Her t-shirt was ragged and old, too large for her small frame, and she wore a pair loose string tied shorts. She paused at once when she saw Lauren. Another dream, this time her vision version of the other was in her nurse's scrubs.

"I bet you can still taste his lips, the warm thoughts of his cool touch on your skin." Lauren was smiling and on the edge of laughter.

"What do you want?" Emily questioned, laying back and letting her head fall into the pillow.

"Is he a better kisser than Colin? I bet he isn't with how close you came to whimper your boy toy's name."

"Shut up." Emily placed her wrist on her forehead. She wanted to wake up. "Why are you here? Why are you always fucking here?"

Emily removed her arm to see Lauren straddling her. "Wonder if the good old boy knew how hot and bothered, he had you, or you had you, I should say, as you barely know country bumpkin. But then I guess he is your type, a good ole country boy with a big heart. How did that work out the last time?" Lauren was still smiling as Emily sat up. "Tell me, all that pent-up frustration you have going on there, why not take it out on someone more knowing? Liam Bell seems like a suitable mate. Or Meara, you know how I like them."

"Never," Emily quickly replied.

"You don't know what you're missing, Red, a little wolf-on-wolf loving is quite exuberating and something you'll never forget." Emily paused as Lauren looked away. "You're not alone…"

Emily quickly sat up in her bed, wide awake in the dark room. "Lauren…" she muttered through a pant.

"I would be curious to know who this Lauren is." Madison appeared from the direction Lauren had been looking in the dream. It wasn't until now that she realized how big the irritating man was. He filled the entire doorway where he stood, blocking out any light that had wanted to come in.

"What do you want?" She tossed the covers off and instantly felt the chill from the open door in the other room. She was wearing the same as she was in the dream. She jumped to her feet and took two steps toward the massive intruder, feeling her claws take shape with each breath.

"Hmm, you and the glorified dog catcher." He smiled, and she could see his enlarged canines in the dim light. He stepped forward, and she could see his yellow eyes. Emily crouched into a position of defense. She was ready to leap at the man no matter how futile the attack would be.

"Have you been spying on me? You can go back and tell your master this is no way to get me to accept his invitation," Emily showed no fear as she stepped a little closer. Madison did not stop as he approached, getting close enough. She could feel the heat radiating off her body. It was then she knew Lauren was right in the dream. It didn't matter; she was sexually frustrated.

"Bell is not my master; I am not a dog to be ordered around. And I can smell the warden on you, on your excitement." He smiled, sniffing at the air between them. "Just like I can smell it now."

"I can too, and I think you need a bath." She smirked and instantly regretted it, she tried to move away from him, but in one swift motion, he pushed her back onto the bed. She growled instantly as she flipped over to the opposite side of the bed. She knew he was too big; she had no plans to stay and fight him, but she would try and outrun him. She hated to think what he would do if he got her pinned down. She could hear his heart racing and smell a musk of arousal coming off the brute.

Emily took another deep breath and looked toward the door as Chamberlain appeared. "We come with no ill intentions, Ms. Meyer, only to invite you out. Far away from anyone who can be harmed where you can be us, wolves unlike the bonfire the other night."

"And if I say no?" Emily replied.

"Then we leave." Madison snarled as he looked back at Chamberlain and then at Emily and nodded, agreeing with the other words.

"I will not shift…"

Madison laughed with a hint of a growl. Before becoming a wolf, she never noticed how subtle a growl could fit into any emotion or gesture. How it would seem to roll into a grouping of words with such ease. "She refused to be who she is meant to be. She can never be part of a pack."

"This is not who I am meant to be!" Emily quickly answered him. She tried to keep her voice down, remembering Meara may be home in her room.

"It is your choice whether you shift or not. We only invite you to meet others. Spend a couple hours with your own kind," Chamberlain said.

Emily paused. She glared at the clock. It said 2 a.m. in red letters. "I need to change." She looked to the door, and Chamberlain turned, walking away.

"You are fine the way you are," Madison said.

"Come, Madison," she heard Chamberlain say from the other room.

"Go, be a good little obedient bitch," she hissed, and the man stopped as he turned. Before she could hear a low rumble coming from the other room. She watched him whimper off, and she shut the door behind them.

"What are you doing, Emily?" She didn't quite understand why she would consistently try and provoke the large man. With each time she encountered Madison, she was sure of one thing, she would have to fight him one day, and there was no way she was going to win that fight. She pulled a pair of dark jeans from the drawer and quickly pulled them on, followed by warm moccasin boots. She tossed the t-shirt to the bed, pulled a simple black one from a drawer, and put it on, followed by a black sweatshirt.

Emily stepped out of the room and saw the two men as they waited outside. She followed. She was even more hesitant when she saw the two Harleys sitting in the driveway beside her truck. But she took a deep breath, being sure to get on Chamberlain's bike. The ride lasted a little over thirty minutes until they pulled off the main road. It was another ten minutes moving slow an old road with a crumbling black top until they came to a mill. Emily regretted it when she saw the number of people. She wasn't sure, but as she approached, there were at least six others there. She recognized Morgan.

"So, what is this?" Emily questioned as she got off the back. Morgan was the closest to her. She recognized Julianne hiding away from the rest of the group and Alma.

"It's your initiation to the pack, little bitch." Emily turned to look at Madison and his mischievous smile. Emily really wished he was not there. She wanted to confront him now, others would see her side of the fight, and she wouldn't have to go at him alone. She really was starting to even hate the man's square-jawed face.

"Leave her alone!" Morgan quickly called, pulling Emily along toward the fire. Emily saw the look on Madison's face before she turned away. She could hear mumbling from behind, but even her sensitive ears could not make out what was said. She looked back to see Chamberlain, Julianne, and Madison walking away in conversation. "Don't worry about them, sugar. You're safe with us." They walked only a few paces as two others greeted them. "This is Marion and Jason."

Jason was a younger man, close to the same age as Emily. He smiled, showing his charming smile. He had a cowboy like appearance, wearing his flannel shirt, jeans, and cowboy boots, only missing the hat to match.

Marion was different. A slender man with a long thick beard and as long hair to match. He was short, but it was obvious it did not affect his confident smile. He was wearing a pair of jeans and no shirt. He was covered in tattoos, she wished she could take the time to admire them all, but she was being pulled along by Morgan.

"How long?" Jason questioned.

Emily couldn't pretend to not know what he was asking. "Half a year." It wasn't quite that long, but she didn't want to take the time to add up in her mind how long she had been a wolf or away from home.

"You can tell. You have the young smell to you." Jason gave a half-crooked smile. Emily felt uneasy and got a laugh from all the others.

The sound of something breaking in the darkness caught all their attention.

"Just a deer." Morgan quickly said. "Tell me." The man was shorter than her as well, something she hadn't really paid much attention to in their earlier meetings, he strolled around, standing by her side, and she couldn't help but get a smell of him. The other night he had smelled of alcohol, almost reeked of it, but now he smelled of sex, she took a moment looking around at the others, but there was nothing that told her who his mate was. "Do you enjoy the hunt?"

"She is still too young," Marion said.

"How long for you?" She looked at Morgan. He had a cocky smile and showed no teeth, but his smile was pure confidence.

"You'll learn, in this pack, I'm a pup," he replied, taking a drink of his beer.

"Six years," Marion said.

"Almost ten," Harrison proclaimed, seemingly appearing away from the rest. She felt a sense of trust in Harrison she couldn't explain.

"Twelve." Jason raised his beer to a toast. Emily looked around for Alma, but the woman was gone as swiftly as Harrison had seemed to appear. Emily took a long deep breath but could not catch her scent.

Emily turned, giving Morgan another look. "Just over two." He smiled. She smiled back; it was interesting having another wolf so close to her in age. She frowned, realizing she was now starting to equate her age to how long she was a wolf instead of her birth year. He seemed so confident in who he was that she wondered if he had complete control and, if so, how? She also couldn't hide her other thoughts, what Lauren had said in her dream about sex with another wolf. "So, to being pups." He reached his beer out in a toast.

"Come," Harrison said as he stood walking away. "Let's leave the two pups to get acquainted. I have a feeling she needs questions to be answered."

"Stay," Morgan said. Emily was surprised when she felt his hand on her wrist, pulling her along into the darkness. She was as surprised when she did not resist following the man who smelled of sex into the black. They walked until the sounds of the others by the fire were drowned out by whispers of the unknown. Morgan stopped them. "There is a stream here. Watch your step." She watched him leap over the small waterway, and she followed suit.

"How long did it take you to gain control?" she questioned.

"I haven't, not fully," he replied. "I still fight it at times; I will admit being around others of our kind has helped." Morgan stopped. He had been slowly walking backward, keeping a look at her. She saw his knowing smile. "You're hesitating; I can understand that as well. I was when I was found by the others."

"Who found you?"

"Harrison, he has been a good guide for me. He isn't as overdramatic as Liam, and he is the co-leader of the pack. It is his rule, the no killing of other humans," Morgan replied.

"And that is why he is here now? And Liam isn't?"

"Liam is in the doghouse, so to say." Morgan smiled.

"Have you killed?" Emily questioned.

"Yes," he replied as he took a seat, and she quickly followed, taking a seat beside him on an old log, "I think most of us have... at least at first, but most of us know it's wrong. We control that hunger; it will always be there. We are predators..."

Emily frowned. "But it can be done," he said.

"I've been having dreams of one of those I've killed," Emily said. "And tonight, it wasn't a dream really, it's like I was awake, and she was there in the room with me. Even warning me about Madison's presence."

"Really freaky, aren't they?" Morgan said. "Harrison has said they are some places between dream and consciousness, that there are those we are connected to through our bloodline and those we've killed. It is like we absorb a part of them." Morgan paused... "You think Liam is a threat to you, I know, but Harrison is here to make sure he sticks to the rule about not killing humans."

"But he already has..."

"He slipped up... I know how that sounds, but we... we can't risk exposing our kind to the rest of the world," Morgan said. "In truth, Liam isn't a threat to you, and I know you are having a tough time grasping that. And you can play it however you want with him. You are your own person even with the pack."

"And Madison… is he a threat to me?" She was thinking about how uneasy she had felt when the man tossed her onto her bed and every interaction they had since they'd met.

"Yes," Morgan bluntly replied. "Madison is a threat, but he is on Liam's leash. He won't act without permission unless he thinks he can get away with it." Emily couldn't help but smile, thinking about how she had called Madison on being Liam's pet and how that must have eaten at him. "Madison has a past that is much more violent than most of the others in the pack; even Liam wouldn't admit it. But we all have a fear of what Madison is capable of. You have more to fear from Chamberlain or Olsen than you do Liam."

"Who's Olsen?" Emily questioned.

"You've met, you may not even realize it… bald, skinny, moves like a creepy little spider always watching…" Emily could see Morgan as he visibly shivered.

"I…" Emily paused; she remembered a bald man that never really grabbed her attention. "Why are they such threats?"

"Maybe Chamberlain has moved past it, but both he and Olsen are former alphas of another pack that are no longer around," Morgan replied.

"What happened to them?" Emily questioned. She felt there was a lot beyond the surface that she didn't know about. She could see Morgan as he was choosing his words more carefully.

"We're the biggest pack in the States, the world, but our numbers are still not large. We have, at times, forced other packs to disband who may pose a threat to exposing who we are. There is a history there that others could explain a lot better than me, I'm still new, and all of this predates even me," Morgan said.

Emily would catch up on it later. She was especially curious about Chamberlain, who she had not picked up as a threat all this time. And now that she knew about Olsen, she would be more cautious and aware whenever she was with others. She needed to pick up on his scent and remember it. She felt at ease with him, there was no pressure in Morgan's presence, and it reminded her of Colin. The way she always felt around her old friend, it did not surprise her that he was gay.

"Come, I have something to help you. Make it easier for you to integrate, make the decision you have weighing you down a bit easier." He took her by the wrist, pulling her along.

Chapter Eleven

Emily followed Morgan, about half a mile from where they had been, and she saw the well-lit home, a couple of vehicles parked on the outside. She walked through the door, directly into a den area. Morgan held the door, letting her pass. She had thought it would be full of other pack members; she at once smelled the presence of normal humans. She saw Jason; his chiseled movie star jaw was sitting closest to the door. She was confused about how he not only beat them there but was already into a game. She even expected to see him in the cowboy hat. She even realized that Marion had made the trip with him. She wondered how long she and Morgan had been talking in the woods, feeling as if only a handful of minutes, though it must have been closer to an hour.

"A new player!" he called out with his big bright smile.

"You're among friends," the woman standing next to him said. Emily saw her and smiled at Alma. For a moment, there she saw someone else. She wore heels with knee-high black socks and a deep purple flowing skirt that reached to the rim of the socks, a white tank top over a black bra. She wore a black cross around her neck that almost got lost in her cleavage caused by her push-up bra. Her hair was as wild and curly as the last time she had seen it, her lips a purple matching her skirt and dark eye shadow with extended lashes. Immediately, the woman reminded her of Ashley. She was a wolf and proud of being so, their eyes met for only a moment and hers were of an unmistakable golden hue.

"What is this place?" Emily questioned.

"We call it the Hive," Julianne said. She had not even noticed the young woman. Her presence caused her to look around the area more feverishly, trying to pick Madison's hulking presence out of the shadows. Emily went as far as to take in a deep breath, but she didn't pick up the brute's scent. "It is sort of where we come to unwind as the youth of the pack." Emily looked around; at least three of the people inside the room were not wolves.

"Everyone here knows about us?" Emily questioned.

"Or course," Morgan said, taking a seat beside another young man, a human. He gave an amusing look to Emily as she continued to look around. "You are truly among friends, no pretense or expectations here."

"We're here to play cards and have fun at least until the moon is high in the sky," Alma said aloud, giving a knowing look around the group, one Emily couldn't help but notice. "This is Alan." She waved to the man next to her with light red hair and stubble. He was human. She also noticed the sly glances between the two. He wore a flannel shirt, and she couldn't tell much more about him. Alma leaned across, grabbing at the pack of cigars before pointing at the next woman, "Bethany, who you know, Bailey, who is the owner of this fine establishment out in the middle of the wilderness." Bethany, she was as familiar with as some of the others, but she didn't quite know whether she should trust her or not.

Bailey, she recognized from the bonfire and as the woman on the other side of Don's radio.

"Nice to meet you all," Emily said. Emily took a seat beside Morgan. "So, why am I here…?"

Morgan smiled as he looked around at the others. "Inclusion, darling." He placed his hand on her upper leg. "You're one of us, whether you like it or not… so it's a matter of making you feel at home around others like you. Trust me, it goes a long way to helping you control your other half when you're with others."

"And I'm sorry for how I may have come across in our first meeting," Julianne said with a big grin. Emily did not trust her, no more than she did her father or Madison. Though if she was to take Morgan's word on it, Liam could be trusted. She had failed to ask her newfound friend about Julianne.

She looked to Morgan's hand still on her leg and smiled as she pushed it away.

"Twenty-dollar limit, ladies and gentlemen," Jason said, starting to shuffle, and he watched as people started to put money on the table and Alma handed chips out. Emily pulled money from her pocket, and Morgan stopped her from paying her way in.

"You're my guest." He smiled.

"It is taken care of," Alma said, getting a look from Morgan. Emily could tell there was a friendship there between those two, and they were the first wolves she had met she truly felt comfortable around. She couldn't explain it with Alma, but she trusted something about her even though they had not met under the best of circumstances.

Emily enjoyed cards. She had played a lot of 'friendly' games with her mom and aunt when she was starting high school, something her dad had frowned upon. She had played some in college, but she blushed when she thought that those were strip poker in a much similar situation to this. It was not until she grabbed a hand holding three sevens in her hand and two kings on the board did she open betting. It went around the table until the final card leaving only Alma, Emily, and Marion in the game.

"How about a side bet?" Alma spoke up. The bigger she smiled, the more she reminded Emily of Ashley. There was wickedness to her smile, filled with Mischievousness. Alma bit her lip, looking at her and then back at Marion. "You. I get a kiss."

"I fold." Emily tossed her cards into the growing stack in the middle of the table.

"Chicken shit," Morgan said.

"It's all right." Alma smiled, looking at Marion.

Marion laid his hand down, showing a full house of threes to go with the two kings. Alma's smile grew. Alma slowly laid her cards out, showing three aces over the two kings.

Emily watched the woman get up from her position three chairs away, circling to where Marion sat next to Emily. "Turn around," Alma said with a smile.

"Bet is a bet." Marion leaned on the table, watching.

The woman sat on his lap, Emily wanted to turn away, but she saw the spark in both of their eyes. They were in love. His smile grew as hers did, her arms wrapped around his neck, barely any room between their bodies as she laid into him.

The kiss was one of passion. Their eyes locked at the moment they were open, and their lips touched.

Emily turned away. She could hear them an arm's reach away. Their breaths grew heavier and heavier. She could hear their hearts thundering; Emily felt her discomfort growing watching them and could tell by others looking away that it was becoming too much.

"A kiss didn't agree to a full-on molestation," Marion said.

Emily turned back. Alma was removing her hands from the man's muscular chest.

Alma smiled as she quickly kissed him on the forehead. "Too bad."

"The moon is out," she heard Jason say.

"Full and glorious and waiting for us to embrace her for a few hours," Morgan said. She could hear the absolute elated happiness in his voice. She wondered if she would ever feel that way about the moon again.

Emily came back into reality as she felt Alma grab her by the wrist.

Alma smiled. "We are going for a run," Alma said, quickly pulling away and dragging Emily to her feet. "And you're going with us."

"What, no!" she quickly proclaimed, stopping in her tracks. Alma never moved. She only smiled.

"You will be with others, you will be with us… you will realize for the first time that this is not the curse you make it out to be," Morgan replied.

This was exactly the reason she had not wanted to come with Madison. Her biggest fear was she would be pushed into transforming into the wolf and having to run with them when she still didn't have full control over that part of her.

Emily could not voice her discomfort with the idea, but she allowed them to drag her along. They piled into an SUV and drove off. From black top to a gravel road leading up behind Bailey's house. Jason had gotten out and unlocked a gate so they could pass. The road went from gravel to dirt with ruts causing them to bounce every time they hit one. They traveled until they topped a peak looking out over a vast wilderness. Emily always thought her time in West Virginia and Kentucky had wilderness, but it was completely different in Oregon. She climbed out of the backseat as Alma turned, pulling her out into the night air. She looked at Morgan, who was amused by the situation.

"Don't be shy." Alma ran her hand down Emily's face. She flinched. She now ran long fingernails down her face, and her eyes shifted to a different color. "We are all animals here."

Of all the werewolves Emily had met before, there was something different about Alma. She could tell this woman had fully embraced what she had become and enjoyed it, which reminded her of Devon. But even knowing that, she still felt safe around her. And Morgan. Emily watched her as she pulled her shirt off, exposing her push-up bra. She turned.

"If you don't mind." She looked back. Her eyes were piercing and full of lust and pleasure. Emily admired the woman's tattoo, another similarity to her former friend though this time, the crow looked as if it was in a fight with a scorpion as the tattoo stretched across the woman's shoulder blades. Emily undid her bra and watched the woman as she turned, letting it fall down her arms. She had small breasts. The bra made them look much larger than they were. Emily watched her as she stepped closer, looking downward, Emily could see the belt wrapped around the schoolgirl skirt. The woman smiled, exposing her large canines. Emily blushed. She was doing this on purpose. Emily reached forward, grabbed the belt, and jerked her closer. "I like it rough."

Emily knew she was a deep shade of red. "I bet you do." She undid the belt and unlatched the skirt, letting it fall down the woman's legs. Emily undid the boots and watched as the woman stepped out of them, then held a leg out as Emily undid one sock and then the other.

"I swear." Emily looked up to see Morgan. She had lost her focus on everyone else and never realized he was there; his bare chest seemed to shine in the moonlight. Ironically, he had a tattoo of a wolf howling at a moon on his upper chest. His pants were unbuttoned, but he hadn't removed them yet or started his change like Alma had.

"What?" Emily questioned. She knew how she looked there on her knees, having undressed the other woman.

"If I had known you would have helped me undress, I would have started my shift early, too." He smiled as he kicked his boots off, then pushed his jeans down his muscular legs. Emily quickly looked around; others were starting their shifts. Julianne, Marion, and Bethany were all in various stages of their transformation. She saw Jason as well on the edge of darkness. This made her look around, wondering if there were other wolves about that she didn't know. Mostly, she wondered if Madison was about, stalking her.

"You're not finished," Alma's voice cut through her. She had lost what she was doing, looking out for others. Emily looked straight into the woman's mid-region. She smiled, realizing the woman still wore her black laced panties. She looked up, watching the woman bite her lips; there was something old about her, more so than even Harrison or Liam, though she could be no older than twenty-five… she was an old soul, and her display of power over her curse was something Emily only could dream about. She gently pulled the woman's underwear down her slender legs and put them carefully on the ground with the rest of the woman's clothing.

"Your turn…" Alma growled. The woman's voice caused her to shudder in fear and excitement. She had never been more than flirtatious with another woman, but this girl, who was likely a couple of years younger, had a power over her she could not explain. The woman ran her finger under Emily's chin and smiled. "You're afraid."

"Terrified," Emily replied, taking a deep breath, and she knew the woman saw her shudder and shake with the breath. There was no hiding her fear of what they were asking her to do. "I have never let…" Emily looked away from her.

"You have never allowed the change or willed it… it has always overtaken you until you've had no choice but to let it happen?" She turned back to look in her eyes. The woman was naked, her eyes had changed back to their chestnut brown, and her sharp canines were gone. Her shift had stopped and reversed in an afterthought, and it caused her heart to race thinking about having that kind of control over what she was.

"Morgan, wait." She looked back at the young man and then at Emily. "We wait." Emily looked at her questioning what the other woman was saying. Emily glared, looking over the woman's body. There were no scars she could see. She glanced around at the others; she could see two fully shifted wolves lingering around each other. It was not long until only the three of them remained there in the fire light with Emily though she could hear the other wolves not far away circling, enjoying the night's air.

"You have never pushed the change," Alma said, taking her hand and pulling at Emily's shirt. There was hesitation, but she relented and let the woman pull it off her and toss it into the pile of clothing.

"Who are you?" Emily questioned with uncertainty. "I don't understand." Emily had not even paid attention to the fact that she was standing there in a bra until the dark-haired woman reached around her body, unlatched it, and pulled it free.

"The world frowns upon women being in charge, let alone the likes of men like Liam or other alpha males being forced to face the fact that a woman can be strong," Alma replied. "With wolves… they still think of an alpha can only have a cock between his legs… but that's a prehistoric view of the world, one for the wolves held in captivity." Emily smiled. "Harrison is different. A lot of the pack is of the opinion that testosterone runs high with male werewolves, and there are others within the pack that if they knew Harrison was a front for a woman, they'd push him out or worse, so someone who I couldn't control would step up and take his place. So, this is understood, this is a secret that stays among us…"

"And the others?" Emily questioned. She looked off into the darkness. "They are close enough to hear what you have told me."

"They are," Alma said as she slowly dropped to her knees, running a hand down Emily's body. A chill went up her spine as she found her way to her jeans. "But as wolves, they are more interested in the run, carried away in their play to pay much attention to those of us who are still untransformed."

"What the…" Emily again shook. The air was cold, she knew, but her skin was on fire. She felt the woman's lips on her stomach above her jeans, sending a chill of excitement down her. She grabbed the woman's hair, pushing her lips away from her bare skin. "Stop that." She heard Morgan laugh, and her eyes darted to the man as he stood there still in his boxer briefs. He was fit in a way she never thought she'd seen on a man before. Every inch of his skin barely masked a bulging muscle. And his briefs left little to the imagination. "What's so funny?"

"You," he replied with a big wide smile. "You're a straight woman, but Alma is turning you on, and you don't know how to react to that."

"Yes…"

"You're maybe doubting your sexuality," she heard Alma's voice, and she looked down at the woman as she felt her tight jeans loosen as the button came undone. Then the zipper.

"Yes… no," Emily quickly proclaimed she wanted to take a step away, and as she did, Alma released her grip on her leg but still head firmly on the rim of her pants.

"It's the wolf." Alma wrapped her hands around the rim of her jeans, tugging them down and exposing her underwear.

"What?" Emily questioned as she took a step forward, placing a hand on the other woman's shoulder. She hadn't even realized she had moved as her other hand ran through her hair.

Alma smiled, pulling her combat boots off, tossing them to the side, and gently pulling her jeans off. Emily obliged with each motion allowing her to undress her. "The wolf doesn't see male or female when it comes to attraction."

"We believe it must deal with why wolves were a common spirit animal to Native Americans, why they saw them as more than killers or scavengers… they saw them as hunters, a pure animal of the hunt… and what is sexuality, to some it is a hunt…" Emily flinched, feeling the other woman's lips again and then her underwear being pulled down her legs. "You're fighting it," Morgan continued with his smile as he approached. She couldn't help but let her eyes drift down the man's body before she bit her lip. She wanted to look away, but she didn't. She didn't know what was happening, her entire being was shifting, and she had little control over it. "Just like you fight the wolf."

She watched him. He was close enough to touch and then closer as he ran a hand down her neck and then leaned in, kissing her on the shoulder blade. She had lost herself completely now. She had stopped paying attention to Alma for a moment, who never quit kissing her. Emily felt the growing hunger inside of her take hold as she gasped and jerked her head up into the air, feeling the transformation coming. She lowered her head; her eyesight had changed. She looked at them as they backed away. Their eyes had changed, yellow as hers, she knew. Morgan finished undressing as well as she dropped to her knees, only her hands holding her off the ground as her back arched and her stomach moved and shifted, followed by her fingers and muscles. It was happening, and she didn't want to fight it. For the first time, she did not resist the wolf. It was why they were coming onto her, forcing her emotions and distractions as the wolf came out.

Chapter Twelve

She growled. She wasn't sure how long it had been since the transformation, but everything felt normal and as it should be here. She'd never felt this as the wolf before. In fact, she could never remember being so conscious during a transformation. This was more than new to her; in the past, she had kept the wolf locked away. She could never remember having this type of control in any shift before. She couldn't help but wonder why this night was different. Did being around other wolves give her that much more control over the other side of her?

She howled. With everything in her, she bellowed out until she couldn't any longer. The echo of other wolves howling grabbed her attention. She was still in the center of the pack, they circled her in all directions, and one after another, they all howled, showing their approval and acknowledgment. They had her back. They were going to keep her safe. They were going to keep others safe from her. She had not seen any since she left the vehicle. She remembered looking at Morgan and Alma as they backed away from her. She remembered growling as she ran off in the wood toward the sounds of others. She howled again as she leaped into the wilderness. Her feet padded the ground, moving faster than she could even believe possible, but still, she did not see them. She chased the sound of movement, growling and snarling but not as a means of threatening. She leaped through the bushes coming upon another. She slid, growling, and the other replied in a growl of its own. She looked closer, realizing it was Bethany. The wolf quickly ran away, and Emily chased. She kept pace a few dozen yards before the other wolf slid to a stop and turned, growling at her. Emily leaped over her, rolling to a stop and looking back at the other. Her heart raced.

Suddenly there were two more with them. She couldn't tell which, but Bethany started running at once, and Emily raced to keep up.

For hours they kept up the same routine, one after another leading the chase through the woods and back. So much so that she had lost track of time as they came to a large clearing. She came to a stop seeing the older man, Harrison, there. Every one of them did. He had flames billowing from a stick of logs. She didn't know what time it was but she could feel daylight approaching.

"Welcome, friends," he said in his gruff voice. Emily looked around as the other wolves began to shift back to human form, but she didn't want to. She growled. "Not what you expected, is it, young one?" he replied with a smile. "Being a part of a family is much different from being alone. And the pack is that a family." She growled again, but she forced the shift back. She was never able to do this before tonight. She never had so much consciousness before as the wolf. It was as confusing as much as it was exhilarating.

Emily sat there, her arms crossed against her bare breasts, others sat around as naked as she, but she was the only one sitting alone and trying to hide from prying eyes. But she had noticed no one was watching. Alma came. Her body seemed to glow in the firelight. "No one is going to force you into doing anything you don't want." She circled, letting her hand drift across her back and shoulders. It was only a second later before she sat down beside her. She held two beers in her other hand, and she quickly reached her the free one.

Emily noticed Bethany and Morgan in an embrace. "He prefers men," Alma interrupted Emily's prying. "But that doesn't mean he doesn't enjoy the soft touch of a woman." Emily took a drink of her beer. "But you prefer men. And I make you uncomfortable."

"It's not…" Emily paused. "I do prefer men." Alma started to move away, but Emily grabbed her by the wrist, stopping her from moving. She continued to try and keep her body hidden from the others. "And you and Marion?"

"He is my fiancé," Alma replied with a smile.

"How old are you?"

"A question for another time," Alma replied. Emily noticed the glare as the woman looked across the fire at Julianne, who stared back at her. "Look around. What do you see?"

"People…" Emily said before she took a moment to look at those who sat around the fire.

"Brothers and sisters," Alma replied.

Emily smirked, giving a look back toward the two who were making out. "If I had a brother, I'm pretty sure I wouldn't be too keen on him grinding me by firelight."

Alma laughed. "You need to get over the past, those you killed, and move forward. Those people who knew you before, you must except that you are now someone different and find a way to live with it," Alma tossed the beer bottle away. Emily watched her get up. The woman was only gone a minute before she returned, sitting back down as Emily finished her own beer.

"Here." The woman's hand was behind her neck, and she could feel her tug her, and Emily did not resist until she was comfortable on the woman's leg. She looked up at her as she tossed the blanket across her naked body, and Emily instantly felt better being covered. The woman stroked her hair. Emily turned until she could see the others. The group had become more than two as several others joined.

Emily woke. She could feel the warm touch of the fire on her skin as she rolled over, only seeing one other there with her. She still wasn't clothed. Alma stared at her with a mischievous smile. She looked older and different now, but it was the same woman she had met the night at the rave.

"Where is everyone?" Emily questioned.

"They are still here," the other woman replied.

"What do you mean…"

"She means you're asleep." Lauren appeared from the darkness.

Emily looked from Alma to Lauren with confusion. "I'm here, and everything that happens here I know of, instantly," Alma replied. "I'm connected to you now."

"How…"

"You wondered if witchcraft was real?" Alma smiled.

"You're a witch…"

"I've studied enough to know the answer to the question you have on your mind," she replied.

"Is there a cure?"

"No," she replied.

Emily pushed herself off the ground. There was no one else around, and the cold bit at her. "What have you done to yourself?" She twisted, looking for the origin of the voice.

"Colin…"

She stood. She was wearing the dress, the same green sundress and knee-high boots she had been wearing the night they were together. She could still remember the horror as it reflected on his face the next morning. "Where are you?"

"Why can't I see you?" She turned in circles, looking for him. He stepped out of the green foliage. She knew this wasn't an Oregon wilderness. This was her back in West Virginia. Emily took a deep breath as her chest shuttered on the edge of tears; she bit her lip, turning not to look at him, but kept looking at him through the corner of her eye. "I'm sorry…"

"Red," he said, stepping further out into the opening. "You have nothing to apologize for."

Emily's eyes were on the edge of tears. She was in shock and couldn't move as he approached. His shaggy short blonde hair, it was curlier than she remembered it. His scruffy beard, darker than the hair on his head, and his piercing blue eyes. He smiled as he stepped closer, a smile of hopefulness without showing teeth. "I missed you, Red."

"I have missed you… you and Ashley so much." He was close enough to touch now, and she was sure she could hear him breathe as he held his arms out to the side, and she leaped into them. He felt real, she knew this was a dream, but he felt real to the beat of his heart in his strong chest. "I missed you, Colin." She couldn't fight the tears off now as they fell down her cheeks clearly.

"Don't cry," he said, her arms wrapped around his neck. She squeezed tightly.

"I needed you."

"You don't need me, never have."

He released his grip, and she fell to her feet. Looking up into his eyes, she quickly looked away, wiping the tears from her eyes. "I did. I've needed you so much… every day, every night…"

"You didn't." She looked back into his eyes. "You were strong enough without me. You have always been strong enough on your own, never needing a man to help you."

"I needed my friend." She frowned.

Colin ran a hand through her hair. It had been so long since she saw him smile. She had never loved him as anything but a friend, but now she ached for him. She again hugged him, he lifted her from the ground, and she snuck a kiss on his cheek before squeezing tightly.

"You ran with them." She felt her own heart stop as she released her grip, and he did the same. She stepped back away from him, looking around as she tried to gather her thoughts.

"I don't…" she replied, biting her lip. "Yes, I did…"

"How did it make you feel?" he questioned.

"For the first time since… I felt alive," she replied.

"You are alive." He frowned, and she looked away from him.

"It's the first time since this happened to me that I didn't hate myself…"

"Why would you hate yourself?" he questioned. She closed her eyes, and as she opened them, she realized they were no longer in the woods. She recognized the cabin. It was the old man's cabin where the final fight with Devon and Lauren took place.

"Colin…" She looked frantically around.

"Why would you hate yourself?" he questioned again, appearing from a back room. He crossed the room, taking a seat in a big reclining chair.

"I…I often wonder why I lived and why God chose to put this on me when so many others in Devon's wake died so horribly. Why did I live?" Emily questioned.

"You've asked these questions so many times, and you know there is no answer, but you can't hate yourself because you lived through that attack," he replied.

"I hate myself because you died," she replied.

"You did not kill me," he replied. She tried extremely hard not to look at him, but her eyes shifted up looking at him, but she could barely see him from across the room.

"If not for me, you'd be alive now… somewhere out there, if I had died that night on the road… you would be alive," she replied.

"But you wouldn't… do you think that would have been all right with me? With Ashley? With your parents?" he replied.

"I might as well be dead to them," she said.

"But you're not, and they know you are not…"

"But they think I ran away, or worse, killed those people and then ran away," she replied.

"Your parents know better, and Ashley in all her bratty ways, has made sure they know this. She has made sure you had to leave for a reason, even if she can't explain to them why. Even if they wouldn't believe the real reasons why you had to leave… they know you did it to protect them." He wiped the tears from her eyes. "You were always so damn stubborn." He smiled, kissing her forehead.

"You used to like that about me," she replied, slowly kissing him on the lips. She felt his hand go through her hair smoothly. For the first time, she missed her long red curls.

"I always liked a lot about you," he answered.

She closed her eyes, pulling him closer. "So much we should have gotten to do together. We, I needed more time. We never had our night… our time together."

"You about tore me to pieces the one time we were together." Emily pushed him back into the chair. She slowly and carefully straddled him, placing her knees on the cushion. She kissed him more passionately as she pushed him further back. She felt his hands, but they were only there for a moment. "I can't stay…"

She sat back on his knees. "…to talk to you again."

"There will be another time," he replied.

"I don't want you to go," she said.

She closed her eyes, feeling his lips on hers for a moment, and she opened her eye. She felt the arms wrapped tightly around her; she was still naked. Alma's hug was tight, she glanced and saw no one else around, but the fire still roared.

"Where is everyone?" she questioned, sitting up. She felt the chill, and for the first time in a long time, it bit at her. She felt the cold in her bones. Her skin was not feverishly hot like it normally was.

"They are gone," Alma replied.

"Where?" she responded.

"Home, mostly," she replied. "Their separate ways."

"Why didn't you wake me?" Emily questioned. Alma ran her hands through her hair.

"You were sleeping peacefully, caught in a dream, were you... it's the first I've seen you have an honest smile," she replied, leaning forward and kissing her on the forehead. "Who was he?"

"He was a friend," she replied, taking a deep breath as she shifted around to face Alma. She pulled the blanket around, pulling it tight around her.

"It seems like with most of us, whoever was closest to us when we turned are those who got hurt or worse," Alma replied, pulling her closer for a hug. Emily fell fast asleep.

Chapter Thirteen

Emily had lost track of time; it had been late morning when she'd gotten home, closer to afternoon, and she had let the day pass her by. She had thrown on a dress, which must have been custom made as it had pockets and a pair of boots. She hadn't seen Meara or heard from her, and when headlights flashed through the nearby living room, she had thought it was her pulling back into the drive. The roar of an engine caused her to open her eyes wide. It was so obviously not Meara's Volkswagen. She rushed to the living room, glancing at the door that was still firmly locked. She grabbed the blanket from the back of the couch and nestled in. She could feel a spring as it poked her in the side, but she didn't want to move. Three loud knocks came at the door, and she took a long deep breath. There was a long pause before the loud knocks came again; this time, five as fast and as loud as the person on the other side of the door could make them.

"What the hell?" She tossed her legs off the couch and pushed the blanket onto the floor. She crossed the room to the door, flipped the peephole open, and quickly shut it, recognizing the man on the other side.

"Open the door, bitch!" Eugene yelled out. "I hear you breathing in there, cow."

"I called the cops. Go home and sleep it off," she replied. He knocked with such force she could feel the door shake with each hit. "Please, just go." Her voice left off with a rasp. "It's not worth it." Emily glared down at the hand that only a second before was on the door, her nails nearly doubled in length.

"Let me in!" he yelled out. "You almost broke my fucking wrist."

Emily took a deep breath, stepped away from the door, and walked to the kitchen's small counter, picking up the phone. "I warned you." There was a pause, a silence where all she could hear was the whistle of the wind outside.

Emily walked back to the door, placing her back to it with the phone in hand. She heard the roar of another engine as she stepped up to the window, looking out. She saw the aggressive guy get in his truck and drive off; it was then she realized it was Don in the other vehicle. She walked to the door opening, stepping out into the cool night air. "I was just about to call the cops."

"I don't think he'll come back now. I threatened his hunting privileges." Don smiled as he walked up to the door. "Couldn't really do that, but he's not all that bright."

"Come in," she said, letting him walk past. She followed, securing the door behind her. She walked over to the couch and sat down, pulling the blanket back up.

"This isn't a booty call, is it…?" Emily smiled, watching Don. Her mind had been drifting with thoughts of Colin in her dream and how the wolf had come to embrace Alma.

"I just wanted to see you, and you didn't answer your phone." She shifted her weight, grabbing at the cell phone and seeing two missed calls.

"I'm sorry."

"No worries," Don crossed the room, taking a seat beside her.

He shifted his head forward, and she leaned in, running a hand down his face and through his beard. "You're graying pretty badly in your beard." She smiled.

"Are you saying I'm old?"

"I kind of like it." She grinned, continuing to run her hand through his thick beard. She twisted on the couch until she lay against him.

Emily woke suddenly, and the home smelled of food. She sat up, noticing she was still in the same dress and even the boots as she put her feet on the floor. The fireplace had a fire burning in it. She wasn't even sure if the chimney was clear enough for one. It was something she had meant to ask Meara but never got around to it. She looked to the kitchen, Don's back was to her, and the smell of bacon filled the air making her mouth water and her stomach growl. "I fell asleep, didn't I…" The last thing she remembered was running her hand through his beard.

Don turned, smiling as he chewed on food. "Your fridge was frightening empty," he said, walking across the room. "I went grocery shopping." He turned, looking back just as Emily eyed the bedroom door close to him.

"You're too sweet," Emily quickly said as she stood. She noticed the window as the curtain was opened to the outside. She stepped up to it, looking at the fresh dusting of snow on the ground.

Don stepped up beside her. She looked at him and saw his big smile. His face shined in the light coming from the outside, he was pale, or it was because of the reflection of snow on his beard.

"What is it?" she questioned, fighting a smile of her own.

"You're beautiful, you know that?" he replied as he ran his hand down the side of her face.

Emily pulled away as their eyes met. "You don't really know me."

"You don't really take compliments very well." He smiled as he turned, heading back toward the kitchen to deal with the bacon. "It doesn't change my opinion, though."

Emily sat at the small kitchen table. "I'm sorry, it's just…"

"Colin." it felt like a kick to her gut hearing his name aloud. She could see by Don's expression that she was ghostly white. "You talked in your sleep and said his name several times. Is that who you're running from?"

She watched him take the bacon from the skillet and put it on the plate with some scrambled eggs and homemade biscuits; he brought them to the table in front of her with his own plate. He turned back, she knew her mouth was still open, searching for words, but none seemed to come to her. "We all have a past, Sarah." He set the cups of orange juice down. "I didn't think you were virginal or anything. And if you want to talk about it, I have been told I'm a good listener."

"Colin…" She looked from Don to the plate of food in front of her. She could see him, a clear picture of her high school friend and the first person she trusted with what she was. "He was a friend."

"To be dreaming about him, I think he was more than just a friend," Don replied as he poked at the eggs, but Emily could see he wasn't really interested in eating. Neither was she.

"He died… rather suddenly," Emily replied.

She could see the horror and sorrow in his face at once. "I'm sorry."

There was a long pause of silence between the two, and Emily stood. She reached behind her, unzipping the dress and letting it fall off her body to the floor, exposing her near-naked frame. Only the red panties and bra remained, and she would have thought the first time she let him see her in her underwear, it would be something uncomfortable but sexy, not these. She wanted to say she handled her friend's death, but she couldn't explain that. She knew the best way to get past this conversation and a future one all the same time. She looked at her shoulder, pointing at the scar and then to her side at the other scar. Don watched. His jaw opened much like hers earlier. She could hear him breathe, trying to think what to say.

"The same animal that did this to me killed him," she replied, and she felt tears begin to well up in her eyes. "I'm not running from him… because he is no longer there. And the person I was before is not the same person I am now. I'm not running from anyone, maybe except for myself. I am just trying to find out who I am and my place in the world."

Don stood approaching, but Emily stuck her hand out, keeping him at arm's length, her eyes shut. She knew they had shifted. It had been months since she had been that honest with anyone. She truly wasn't running from her past life. She was trying to find her place in the world. She felt him graze past her hand, and in that moment, the warm touch of her arms engulfed her, pulling her in tight, and she instantly wrapped her own arms around him, hugging him.

"I don't know who I am anymore… am I Sarah… am I Emily…" A lump caught in her throat, saying her real name aloud to him. "Months ago, I was a lawyer's assistant. My biggest worry was if I would have to get my daily run in before or after work or if it would be the middle of the night before I could put my running shoes on and just run. Because that is when I felt the most alive…" Don squeezed her just a little tighter, and the tears began to fall as she felt her legs go weak, and she knew the only reason she was still up right was he was holding her. "I want to go back to being normal."

"Hey, hey." His large hands pulled away from her, but she didn't want to release, and it took everything in her to put weight back on her legs to look up at him. He kissed her on the forehead. "Everything will be okay. Things have a way of working themselves out."

Emily smirked. "Not with me. Not with what my life has become." He kissed her on the forehead again. He was still a stranger, and though she wasn't telling him her secret, she was pouring her heart out to him.

"This is a terrible second date." He laughed.

Emily did as well as she pulled back close to him. She could hear his heartbeat through his chest. Steady and calm. "You did at least get me in my underwear," she replied.

"And it ends with you crying, doesn't say much about me, does it?" Her arms were again wrapped tightly around him, and he pulled her close as they seemed to breathe as one.

"I need to take a shower." She laughed, pulling away and trying to get some composure. She wiped her eyes clear as she turned to pick the dress up, leaving him there. She had thought about inviting him along, but didn't.

The water was scalding. She could hear nothing over the sound of it pouring over her. Her head started to hurt. It had been as if the world had been lifted off her shoulders. She exited the shower grabbing a simple white t-shirt and shorts, forgoing underwear as she wanted to get back to him. She exited out into the living room, and half expected him to be gone. "You're still here?"

"My momma always told me never leave a girl crying, distraught, and in her underwear…"

"Why would you momma talk to you about women in their underwear?" She flopped back onto the couch, pulling her legs up. She could see it had started to snow harder outside.

"Awkward," he replied with a smile as he crossed back from the window and sat down beside her. Emily crossed her legs over his as he sat. She ran a hand through her short hair, and for the first time in a while, she found herself missing her long red locks, just like in the dream with Colin. She watched him; he had a chiseled chin even through the beard and a strong mouth with thin lips. She felt his hand tightly grab her wrists and pull her toward him, and she didn't resist as she found herself straddling him, arms wrapped around his neck as she looked into his eyes. "Do I call you Sarah… or Emily?"

"Emily." She smiled.

"It is nice to meet you, Emily."

"It is nice to meet you too." Her smile grew. It was an honest, happy smile, even if just for a moment. Her eyes shifted from his eyes to his lips and back, and she tightened her legs against his legs. "It's been a while, and I don't know if I'm ready," she lied. She was more than ready. She just wasn't sure if she could control the other part of her in the excitement. She knew she had to be careful with him. She slowly leaned in, kissing him on the lips, her forehead against his.

"It's okay. We don't have to," he replied, kissing her again.

Emily shifted her weight as she got up, pulling Don up to his feet in the process.

"I'm sorry… it's just…" She started to say more, but he cut her off.

"You don't have to make excuses with me," he replied. "You never have to make excuses with me." He leaned forward, kissing her on the forehead before he grabbed his things and left.

It had been raining for a while when Emily left work. Heading for her truck, she saw the flower sitting on the windshield before she ever got to it. She could smell Liam on the rose, a white rose, and she tossed it to the wet pavement. "Someone has an admirer." She turned to see Chloe. This was starting to remind her of Nebraska and the customer who had been getting too comfortable with her.

"It's nothing." Emily could smell the sweet perfume on the woman. She was wearing six-inch heels, a short skirt with stockings, and a shirt that showed off her cleavage.

"I'm going to pick Allison up, take her out for a couple drinks. You want to come along?" Chloe questioned. Emily gave her a curious look. "I'm not a complete bitch, you know." It had become obvious with their limited interactions that Chloe was never going to recognize her as the woman from the night at the gas station.

"Okay," Emily replied, putting her keys away and joining the woman in her own vehicle.

It was a short drive to Allison's. Chloe led them up to the door. She knocked three times with no answer. "Her car is here," Chloe said.

"She's here." Emily could hear her crying, the soft whimper as she cried into a pillow.

"How can you tell?" Chloe questioned.

"I just know." Emily stepped up to the door knocking louder and louder. "Allison, we know you're home. Let us in." Emily could hear movement. She stepped back away from the door, and Chloe remained next to it. The door barely crept open, it was pitch dark on the inside, and she barely got close enough to let the others see her.

"I don't feel like going out," Allison said.

Chloe turned to block Emily's view. "But you said."

"Let us in, Allison." Emily pushed Chloe to one side, and she could hear Allison sigh. "Please, let us in."

"What's going on?" Chloe questioned. Emily was against the door now. There were too many emotions now, from everything that was going on with Liam, her conversation with Ashley, and the pack, plus Don. She was being torn in several different directions, and she could smell the other man's sweat on Allison. She could smell the fresh scent of blood.

"Let us in, Allison," Emily said again.

There was a momentary pause before she shut the door, and Emily could hear it being unlocked. It was only a minute before it opened, and Emily could see the bandage on

Allison's face. Her clothes were ripped, and Emily rushed through. "What the hell?" she heard Chloe say.

"Did he rape you?" Emily could smell the strong scent of sweat on her.

"No," Allison replied with a frown.

"Where is he, Allison?" she quickly questioned.

"He'd be at the bar." She turned to look at Chloe. "It's where all the redneck drunks go. It's a very roughneck crowd."

"Lock the door, and don't you let anyone else in until we are back," Emily said as she turned to look at Chloe. "Take me."

Chloe gave her a shocked looked. "We should call the police, Sheriff Bell."

"They're obviously not going to do anything," Emily replied. "So, take me..."

"It's a bad crowd." Emily could see the fear on the young girl's face.

"If you don't take me, I'll go by myself," she admitted. She wanted Chloe to go, to have someone there who she could use as a centering point. To keep herself calm enough not to let the wolf out but still put the fear of god into the man.

"Okay."

"Lock the door behind us." They exited the home, and Emily stayed by the door a moment to make sure Allison did just that.

It was a short drive to the bar. Most of the ten vehicles out front were run-down, beat-up trucks, much like what Emily drove. She exited, rushing toward the door with Chloe right behind her. "This is a bad idea," she heard Chloe say just before she reached the door.

"Just stay behind me." They walked through the door, and the smells of sweat, beer, and urine were strong enough that it took Emily's breath away.

Instantly she heard a whistle. "Boys, it looks like the entertainment has arrived."

"I have dibs on the blonde." Emily could hear Chloe's gasp. "She has nice tits. Look at those things."

"Wait outside," Emily said, looking around the bar and immediately regretting bringing Chloe along. It made her as much of a target as herself.

"I won't leave you alone in here," Chloe said.

Emily looked around until she saw him sitting on a bar stool. She rushed forward. She was only a few paces away when he looked at her. "It's the little ginger bitch from Rosie's. I wish you would have opened your door so we could have had a private… moment before your boyfriend showed up."

Emily kicked the stool, and it flung out from under him. He fell, hitting his head on the bar and then to the floor. Emily stomped on his closest wrist, and he screamed out in pain. She looked around. None of the other men in the bar were rushing to help him. They all had confused looks on their face. "You are a fat, disgusting bastard."

"Bitch, I think you broke my hand!" he screamed out at her.

"You stay away from Allison. Do you hear me?" She stood looking around. She left him for only a second grabbing the old knife from the bar. Even the bartender was just watching her, not moving quickly to stop her or call the police. She came back, he was grabbing at his hand, and she quickly kicked him in the side with a loud groan. She leaned down, putting the knife to his face.

"Sarah, I think we should go," she heard Chloe say.

Emily ran the knife down the side of his face, barely breaking skin. She wanted to do it with her fingernails. She knew her eyes had shifted, her nails were longer, she wanted to gut him, and she growled. "Everything from here on out you do to Allison, I do to you." She tossed the knife to the floor and backed away. She looked around at the others.

"Crazy bitch," one of the men said.

"Bet she is a fun fuck," another said as she backed into Chloe, pushing her back toward the door.

"Bet she cuts your balls off after she is done," a third said just as they reached the door. Chloe ran to her car, but Emily only walked. She looked back at the door where only one man stood watching as they drove.

"That was fucking crazy," Chloe said with excitement in her voice. "You're crazy, Sarah." Emily only looked out the passenger side window. She could see the reflection of her yellow eyes looking back at her. "You're a complete badass."

"Stop the car," Emily muttered.

"What?"

"Stop the car, please," Emily looked at Chloe. She couldn't help herself, and she could see the horror on the other woman's face as she slammed on her brakes. Emily opened the passenger door, and she crawled out into the bud, unable to stand. Several feet she crawled forward before she threw up. Her entire stomach lurched. She felt the wolf; it wanted out. She threw up again as she felt Chloe looming over top of her as she tried to push herself up off the ground but was unable to. She felt the other woman's hands on her shoulder. "Get off me," she growled, swiping at Chloe.

"What's wrong with you?" she heard her ask as she rolled over onto her back, trying to catch her breath. She felt the mud cling to her, the other woman staring down at her as she lost consciousness.

Emily woke suddenly. She was undressed except for a t-shirt in an unfamiliar bed. "Hello?" she called out.

"You had me worried sick." Allison appeared from another room. "Chloe said you were throwing up…"

"Where is she?"

"She had to work this morning," Allison replied. "She undressed you, washed you off… you were covered in mud. I washed your clothes." Emily sat up, pushing the shirt so it would cover her as she flipped the blanket off her. Allison sat down beside her. "She told me what you did to Eugene as well… you didn't have to do that."

"Someone did," Emily replied.

"Thank you," Allison said as she stood leaving the room, it was only a moment later before she returned with Emily's clothing.

"I need to go home," she replied.

"I'll take you to Rosie's. My shift starts in a little bit, anyways," Allison said with a smile as she left Emily alone with some privacy.

Chapter Fourteen

Emily quickly rushed home. She was surprised to see Meara's car in the driveway. She rushed through the door to her room, and she quickly heard Meara coming in her direction. "Late night?"

"I crashed at Allison's," Emily replied.

She walked over, taking her place next to Emily on the bed. "You should come with me, check my studio out."

"Your studio?" Emily questioned.

"Yes," she replied with a smile walking back to Emily, taking her by the wrist and dragging her along. She had no reason to say no, and the woman never gave her a chance to say anything as she pulled her away to her car. The small two-story building was on the opposite end of town from the house they rented. It was off to itself, and she had never even seen this part of the small town.

Meara unlocked the door. "This whole place is yours?" Meara looked back at her with a smile as she forced the door open and turned on the light on the inside.

The inside had new drywall hung and in the coating process, but it was mostly one large room with a counter and shelves surrounding the outside of the room. "This was my dad's garage at one time. I paid some men to hang the sheet rock but leave the doors because I like the way it looks. I'm doing the dry wall myself and painting. I think when it's done, I'll turn this into a yoga studio." Emily could see the excitement of someone who knew what they wanted to do with their life in Meara's smile.

"So, this is where you disappear to all the time. Yoga?" Emily said with a nod.

"Yeah, why?"

"Namaste." Emily walked up to the counter.

Meara followed. "I figure I can work out a set schedule with Rosie… and use my open hours beyond that."

"So, you're going to hold down a full-time job and run your own business? Sounds like a lot of work," Emily implied.

"Yes, and I could probably use some help if I knew someone who would work cheaply, maybe a friendship discount," Meara replied as she jumped up, sitting on the counter. "Not to mention the upstairs has a small apartment, two beds, one bath… not all that much different from what we are renting now."

"Maybe free classes and some of that tea you mentioned the other day," Emily said as she turned to put her back on the counter. "I could use some calming presence in my life." She thought about the past few days and the panic attack she had the night before; she would give anything to have a full night's sleep without it being the effect of a transformation.

"If I was to ask you for some basics on yoga… mostly as I try and find a way to relax, what would you suggest?" Meara leaned over the counter, grabbing two mats and putting them under her arms. She grabbed Emily by the wrist as she pulled her toward the center of the room.

"Sit." Meara set a mat, and Emily did as she suggested. "Just like me." Meara crossed her legs under her placing her wrists on her knees. "This is a meditation pose, mostly for relaxation. Before you start yoga, the most important thing you must do is learn to relax your mind and body." Emily snorted.

"What?"

"Neither of those have been easy for me of late, especially relaxing my mind," she replied.

"That is what this is all about, getting control of both mind and body. Learning to relax and control who you are and want to be," Meara said. "You must keep the negative out, all that bothers you… put a wall up between you and it. You are the one in control of yourself. Not the wolf, the wolf may be a part of who you are, but you are the one in control."

Emily held the pose longer than she thought. She just sat there breathing and thinking. Feeling her own body. She opened her eyes to see Meara sitting closer to her with a big smile on her face. "What?"

"You did well. Of course, that is only meditating. The actual yoga exercises will not be quite as easy," she replied with a smile.

Emily looked at the simple clock hanging on the wall. "I think I need to go."

"Sure," Meara said.

The two of them got ready and headed out the door. Emily stopped as they exited. Chamberlain leaned back against his bike with his arms crossed against his chest. This was the first time she'd seen Chamberlain since her conversation with Morgan. She didn't know if she saw the man any different, but she could see him as an authority figure, an alpha, as they liked to say. There was a confidence about the man that she couldn't deny.

"Ladies," he said with a big smile.

"Chamberlain," Meara said. Emily shouldn't have been surprised, but she was as she looked from her new friend to the man as he nodded at Meara.

"Bell wants to invite you both for dinner." He smiled, and Emily sighed as her heart raced, and she felt Meara's hand grab her wrist. She then looked at her.

"Yes, we will," she replied quickly for them both. Emily felt a lump in her throat. She couldn't speak. This was conniving on his part, knowing he would have her cornered by inviting a friend to come along as well. And especially a friend who knew their secret.

"Then say… seven. Don't be late." He mounted his bike and fired it up. She watched as he roared off, kicking gravel from the cold ground in the process.

Emily knew she had lost all color when her eyes met Meara. "What's wrong?"

"What do you know about Bell?" she questioned, her hand balled up into a fist. The abrupt meetings were becoming too much for her. "Besides the obvious."

"I know he lives in one of the biggest houses in the valley, he comes from one of the oldest families in the region, and he comes and goes. He doesn't spend a lot of time here, but when he is here, he throws elaborate parties and bonfires and is highly active in the community. Plus, now that I know he is some sort of supernatural alpha wolf… I want to see the inside of that house even more." Emily could see the excitement on Meara's face. It was a vastly different kind of excitement than what she had when she talked about her future business. "You're going, and I will not take no." Again, she felt the other woman's hand on her wrist, dragging her off toward the car. "I have a dress you'd look amazing in."

Emily was not surprised to see the Bell home was off the beaten path. They approached the large gate with brick platforms on each side. Emily snorted. "What?" Meara questioned, looking over at her from the driver's seat.

"I half expect to see a little thin man in a dark hood wisp out and open the gate like out of some horror movie," Emily replied. She knew the real horrors were inside, waiting for them. The gate crept open in front of them, and Meara pulled up the drive. They parked at the end of the large drive, near a water fountain with a large wolf standing over top of other wolves, and Emily stared for a long time.

"It's beautiful," Meara proclaimed, "but takes on a whole new meaning with everything I know about the man now."

"He fancies himself the pack master in every way," Emily announced.

"That he does." They turned just as Julianne stepped out of the door.

"Good evening, ladies." They turned to see Liam Bell standing in the doorway. "If I had known the two of you were going to dress so formally, I would have done so myself." He wore only a pullover long-sleeved shirt, and jeans. Emily noticed immediately the man was barefoot. He stepped out in the cold and greeted them at the bottom of the formed concrete steps. "Dinner will be ready shortly." He took Meara by her hand and kissed the back of it, the entire time he glanced up at Emily. The regret in her stomach grew; this was more than just a simple mistake. He took Emily by her hand and did the same.

"I have a nice evening planned for the both of you," his grin grew until it seemed to consume most of his face. "I feel like I owe you both sincere apologies for past events, and maybe I have misrepresented myself."

"Why, thank you, sir," Meara said. Emily only nodded as she focused on him again.

"Please, call me Liam. We're all friends here." He stepped to the side, letting the two of them walk past. Emily was the first of the stairs and through the double front doors. Past the front door, the room opened into vaulted ceilings with a winding staircase. "My family home."

"It's beautiful," Meara said.

Emily felt Meara's elbow poke her in the ribs, and she dropped her attention to the long stairway and looked back at them, "Yes, it's... beautiful." The room had oil paintings hanging everywhere, offsetting the room's pale white walls. The floor was cherry hardwood with three-piece crown molding linings on the ceilings and a tall baseboard on the floors. Emily saw the large glass chandelier next. It was five feet in width and seemed to float above them. She was not lying. It was beautiful.

"I will gladly give you a full tour after dinner, if you don't mind. This way."

He showed them to the left of the home's main entrance through a small hallway to a dining room. There was a small, intimate table in the middle of the room with white linens and three-place settings. Emily half expected a large oak table that would have fit naturally in some medieval castle. "I've got some trout, some fresh veggies, and wine. We can never forget the wine." He clasped his hands together with a slight bow as he turned and walked away toward what Emily suspected was the kitchen.

Emily turned to survey the dining room. "You can at least pretend you're happy to be here." She turned back to Meara.

"Sorry, it's just…"

"You don't trust easy, I get it. And I understand… but what is he going to do, murder us?" Meara said with a smile. "Besides, we already know what it is he is."

"You're right." *Or worse. He could turn into a werewolf, kill you, and force me to turn as well,* was the second thing she wanted to say. "I will try," she retorted, turning back to look at the room. She slowly walked over to a nearby door looking into the nearest room. It was a library. There was a big oak desk sitting near the windows with maps and dozens of papers sitting out in the open.

Emily stepped further into the room with Emily right behind her, "I don't think we should snoop."

"He shouldn't have left the door open," Emily replied. The office looked typical, with lots of books, framed diplomas, and articles; nothing seemed out of place. One thing grabbed Emily's attention the most as she walked forward. A painting, it was beautiful, but the content sent a chill up Emily's back. A large black wolf stalked its prey, with blood dripping from its jowls and a woman with long red hair as she tried to crawl away from him. Her eyes were as yellow as the wolf's, and she could tell it was freshly painted.

Liam's voice broke her concentration. "The painting is called 'The Alpha and his Mistress'."

Emily splashed cold water on her face. Her reflection was pale and as horrified as she felt her stomach churn in distress. "He is trying to bait you," she said, taking a deep breath as she smiled at her own reflection. She came out of the room and entered the dining room to see them sitting. They both turned as she entered.

"I hope everything is okay?" Bell questioned as Emily took her seat.

"Everything is fine," she replied with a smile.

Meara stood. "I need to visit the little girl's room."

Liam stood in politeness as she left the room. "I take it you did not appreciate my painting."

"Is it a threat?" she quickly asked, looking back to make sure Meara was gone.

"A threat, no, not in the least, Ms. Meyer," Liam said with a big grin. "Stand, walk with me." Emily did as he asked. As they exited out of the room, through a small hallway into another room, and to some big glass double doors, he opened and stepped out into the night air. He shut them behind as Emily walked out. He walked up to the edge of the balcony, looking out over the forest. "You have met the majority of the pack. Your honest thoughts?"

"About?"

"Joining, becoming one with us…" Liam questioned.

"I still don't know," Emily replied.

"I wish I could persuade you. Convince you the hunter was an accident," Liam said, turning to look at her. His eyes were light blue, and there was an ease to them. She had not realized it, but her stomach had stopped churning as she tasted the cool air.

"Of course, the painting does not help your case," Emily said.

"A case of misguided inspiration, I assure you I meant nothing of it. Not in the least as a threat," he replied. He smiled, showing no teeth. He was arrogant and charismatic at the same time. Emily could see how others could fall for his charm, but she knew men like him, she had fallen for men like him. She had a taste for the bad boys, and he was all of that and more. He was like her. "You must give me a chance to prove myself."

"Start by stopping the surprises… no more 2 a.m. visits from your henchmen. Keep Madison as far away from me as possible," he smiled.

"He does have a way to get under people's skin," he replied. "No more surprises. Honor among wolves."

"Thank you," Emily replied. She was relieved at the idea of keeping Madison away from her.

"But I ask one favor of you as well," he replied with a smile. "On the next clear night, you come and run with me as the wolf this time."

Emily sighed. "It is a promise." She didn't know why she made the promise.

The doors opened behind them as Meara stepped out into the cold air. "It's freezing out here, and it doesn't seem to be bothering either of you."

Liam approached Meara putting his coat around her. "Ladies, I hate to cut the dinner short, but I have been called away on some urgent business. Feel free to take your food along with you and let yourself out when you are ready."

Emily allowed Meara to take her food as well as they approached her car. She realized Meara still had Liam's jacket. "His jacket," Emily said.

"I know. It gives me an excuse to come back tomorrow," Meara replied.

"I know you're curious, Meara, but I don't want you getting too close to him… to us…" Emily quickly said.

"I'll be careful," she replied. "Trust me."

Chapter Fifteen

Emily pulled into work after nearly being late the next day. Emily smiled, walking to the small employee lounge, and saw a dozen flowers in the cheap vase with a small box of chocolates sitting beside it. She felt ill. Even from this distance, she could smell Liam on them.

"From my dad?" she turned to face Meara.

"No card. Who else?" Emily lied. "Did Liam call you about the jacket?"

"Not yet." Meara showed her fingers crossed with a smile.

Emily's day went by fast. She couldn't wait to get off and planned to surprise Don at work. She knew Allison would be in soon. She watched the clock feverishly. An hour passed, and still, her relief had not shown.

"Allison isn't coming," Rosie said with a half-smile. "I just got a call; she is in the hospital. You can take off. We can handle the rest of the evening."

Emily walked through the hospital doors. Unlike the one back home, which was a large complex, the one in the town was only three stories tall.

"Allison Haze?" she questioned at the counter. The nurse gave her a look of sorrow, and Emily's heart sank as she stepped back from the counter. She turned to see Chloe holding a young kid not far away. She never realized until now how close Chloe and Allison may have been. When Chloe saw her, she instantly looked away, and tears began to fall. "What happened?" Emily questioned as she reached her.

Chloe stepped away. Emily could tell it was Allison's kid. It was only a moment before she returned, dragging Emily away from the hospital. "I came to pick her up. We were going to go see her ex this morning, see if I could get him to take her in for a few weeks… she was unconscious when I got there." Chloe was having a challenging time breathing. "She never made it to the hospital." Emily hugged her, pulling her close. Emily wanted to scream but didn't as she squeeze the younger woman tighter. Emily realized that she was holding Chloe upright, the only reason the younger woman was still on her feet.

The first place Emily stopped was the bar. She walked through the door and could see only two people there. "Can either one of you tell me where Eugene Roberts is?"

"So you can beat his ass again?" She glanced at the one who did not speak; he was passed out with his head on the table. She walked over to the bar tender, the same one from the other night.

"He killed her. That degenerate bastard killed her," Emily growled, grabbing him by his collar and pulling him close to the bar. "Do you know where he is?"

"He… he… will be with his drinking buddies up at the cabin off the interstate… Fern Drive…"

Emily had parked two miles away after she passed Fern Drive, finding a small off-road where her truck would not be seen. It all felt like a blur to her everything happened so fast from the time she left Liam's the night before till now as she walked up the drive. She pulled the hood over her head, but she could smell him. It was the edge of dark, and her heart raced. She was strong enough to confront him without the wolf, to hurt and threaten him if he ever touched her again, but that was the night before. Now she had other plans. She knew that when she hid her truck. Smoke bellowed from the chimney, and two other vehicles were in the drive beside the abusers.

"Can I help you, miss?" An overweight man poked his head around the truck, he had a shotgun leaning over his shoulder, and her pulse quickened.

"Is Eugene Roberts here?" she questioned.

"He is inside. Can I ask who is calling?" he questioned. He wore overalls, and they were covered in stains and mud.

"It's all right, Chris." He stepped outside of the cabin, and there were two other men following him. They all looked the same to her, wearing camouflage. Stained and dirty. One, a skinny man she was sure weighed less than her, had tobacco juice running down his face. "She is the night's entertainment." He approached, and Emily clinched her fists. "Hope you don't mind. You'll be pleasing four of us, and I get to go first."

He laughed.

She growled.

"Oh, we have a feisty one, always the most fun," the fourth man spoke.

"You guys know what he did to Allison?" Emily questioned. The four of them looked to him and then to her and only laughed and smiled.

"Of course we do." One snorted.

"She had it coming," another said.

"Bastards," Emily said, glaring at the one she knew deserved it the most.

"Play nice," he said with a smile just before he finished off his beer and smashed it on the ground. "Or you'll get much, much worse than my girl did. You're not going to take me by surprise tonight."

"This doesn't concern any of you," Emily said, looking at the other three men.

"You're right. No one has to get hurt, so just let us have what we want," the skinny one declared, rushing forward. There was no hesitation in her movement as she slapped him down. The man wailed away, even falling to the ground. The other three men roared out in laughter.

"Told you she was feisty, little minx… I bet she fucks like a wildcat!" the largest of them called out.

"I bet," another laughed. Emily lowered her head, taking a deep breath.

"Fucking bitch!" the skinny one screamed out, and quickly, the others saw why he had shrieked, his face covered in blood from four long scratches along his cheek cut completely through his jaw.

"Oh, you've done it now whore!" the one she wanted most called out.

The largest of them set the gun down and ran toward her, he had intended on tackling her, but she dodged easily, reaching out and racking her hand across his chest in motion.

It was instantly he started screaming. "Fucking bitch ripped my nipple off!"

She looked back. Her eyesight was blurred. She knew her eyes were completely yellow and shifted. But she was still in control. Her anger and hatred of these men were keeping her in control. She had ripped through his jacket, shirt, and chest, exposing flesh. She glanced at her hand and long fingernails.

She turned back, looking at the only one of the new strangers she had not marked. "You can still leave." He looked from the abuser, the one she had come here for, and back to her.

"Fuck you," he charged. Emily knew she had to kill them all. She felt her hand slice through his throat like butter. There were no screams, only the gurgle. She leaped to her main prey knocking him to the ground. She twisted her head to look at him. He was pale as a ghost and whimpering.

"Please, don't kill me."

"Did Allison beg?"

"What?"

"When you were beating her, you piece of shit, did she beg?"

"Yes," he muttered through tears. She looked up to see the large one holding his chest had reached his gun. She moved on instinct, two quick steps, and she leaped, knocking him onto the hood of the car at his back, her legs pinned his arms across the car.

"Pigs, you're not men." She slashed a cut into his forehead.

"Please don't kill me," he muttered in fear.

"I won't." She twisted off him, hearing the footsteps of another coming up on her. The skinny man brought the ax down into his friend's chest, and Emily twisted her head, looking at the man as he fell back, scooting away from her, leaving his weapon cleaved into his accidental target, and smiled. She had kept her promise not to kill him.

"What the fuck are you?" the skinny man questioned. He scooted backward away from her, blood pouring from his cheek. She slowly stalked after him, and as she reached him, she saw his jeans become wetter.

"Disgusting."

"Please don't kill me," he muttered the same words as the fat man.

"Why shouldn't I?" she questioned. "You tried to murder me with an ax." She took two steps forward; leaning over him, she twisted his cheek so she could get a good look at her work.

"Please." His lips moved, and no sound came out, but she knew what he tried to say.

"No." She slashed.

Emily looked up and sighed. He was gone. The reason she had come here. The reason she had let the wolf out, the man had run away. She glanced to the cabin, the door still open as she lifted her head up into the air to get a scent of her prey, and she picked it up instantly. A mix of beer, sweat, and urine, and she could hear him as he rushed through brush and even as he fell to the ground. She wondered for a moment feeling the adrenaline take her over, *was this what Devon felt the night he had attacked her.* Emily wanted to laugh and call Eugene's name but instead she howled.

She stalked him through the wilderness. The wolf wanted to hunt, not her. She was aching, her stomach cramped with each step. She fell to the mud. She could hear him not far away whimpering. She growled and snarled as she tried to shake off the change. It was strong. She rose, sitting on her knees, glaring up at the moon, and howled. The whimpering grew as she fell forward again.

"No," she muttered and smiled. "He is my kill…"

She felt herself lose her breath; she could not believe what she was saying. Images of Allison flashed through her mind. Beaten, bruised, and dead because of him the night before, and now she was dead. "Mine."

She stumbled to her feet, moving forward, trying to focus on him, but it was becoming foggy now as the wolf was gaining more control of her body.

Again, she growled, "Come out, come out wherever you are." Her voice was hoarse. His whimpering grew louder, and she shifted her position and the direction she faced. "It takes a small man to hit a woman, not a man at all."

A pathetic slug who is going to get what he deserves," she growled, and she could smell the strong scent of urine grow. "Disgusting pig… that is what you are, swine." She crept forward; step by step, she could hear his breathing grow clearer. Until she saw him, huddled with his back to a tree, pistol in hand. "Had a weapon all along, and yet you would not stay and help your poor, poor friends as I ripped them to pieces," she growled.

"What the hell are you?" he questioned. His hand shook: he was having a problem holding the gun in the air, she saw as she tilted her head from side to side.

"I'm death," she said, smiling, exposing her enlarged canines, and she saw the true sight of fear on the man's face. "Did she beg as you beat her, Eugene? As you threatened to take her life? I want to hear what you said to her as she begged for her life."

"Stay back," he whimpered.

"Tell me, what did you say to her when she begged you not to hit her again," Emily replied as she took a step forward, and he pulled the trigger, and only a click of an empty chamber. She leaped, knocking the gun from his hand as she leaned down over him. "Shooting blanks, I bet it's not the first time for you."

"Please," he muttered.

"I have no doubt she said it often as you beat her," she replied, standing up and getting a clear look at the moon above. "I was in an abusive relationship once… he never hit me. Nothing that brutal. But he treated me like shit. Cheated on me. Talked down on me. My parents and my best friend saw it, but I kept going back to him, even now, I don't know why I kept going back to him." She lowered herself back down, putting her finger on his chin and making him look at her. "Why is it we keep going back?"

His lips quivered.

"Oh, you're afraid of saying what you are thinking. I am sorry," she muttered. "Say it… it doesn't matter. I'm going to kill you anyway."

"You're weak."

Emily laughed as she sat down on his legs. "Eugene, Eugene, Eugene, we're not weak. People like you are weak," she replied, slowly moving her finger down his chest, the nail cut slowly through skin, just enough to cause a trickle of blood. She stopped when she reached his belly button and then brought her attention back to his face. "I had a friend once; he would have made a great boyfriend… husband…

father. But he died because of what I am. And now, Don… he's sweet. I honestly don't know much about him, but he seems sweet, romantic, and a lot like Colin. I'm half the mind to run again. Find some other place to hide from what I am. But I'm tired, tired of being alone. And then there is the pack… others like me, a way I can be who I am and not be alone…"

"Please," he muttered again.

"You're pitiful." She slashed through him, her eyes half open. She continued to wail at him with open claws. She couldn't see what it was she was hit, but she felt it, flesh, bone, and tendon. She just kept striking him long after he stopped screaming.

Emily opened her eyes in horror, remembering what she had done the night before. She rolled over onto her hands and knees and retched several times before she sat up on her bare knees. She realized she was naked, covered in mud and blood. She looked around. She had no idea where she had ended up. She could see everything the wolf did as it ran. Its hunger for death satisfied, she only ran and chased other animals, running alongside an elk as it whined in terror at the beast at its side, but she did not kill it until she was bored. She retched again just before she stood up in a stumble. Her muscles were weak; she could feel the soreness creep in from how much she had run.

"Fucking stupid, Emily." She looked around, and it was all coming back to her now. She could smell the direction she had traveled the night before; she wasn't utterly lost.

"I remember this." Emily jerked around.

"Fuck," Emily muttered. Lauren stood there smiling.

"The first time I killed because I wanted to…"

"What are you doing here?" Emily questioned, turning. "Am I sleeping still…?"

"No, I'm here with you, sweetie, walking this path of blood, death, and gore… you really did a number on those men… you played with them. Whatever possessed you to do such a thing?" Lauren questioned.

"Swine," she muttered.

"Oh, this is about the little blonde girl, isn't it? Pitiful thing, a life cut so short. So violent and protective, Ashley would be proud of the poisonous flower you are blooming into, full of dangerous sharp thorns." Lauren snorted.

"Shut up." Emily glanced back but never stopped her forward progress. "What did I do?" Emily paused, turning back to her apparition. She looked so life-like. Emily knew she was awake and not dreaming. The setting was new to her. This is where she curled up the night before and slept.

"Look around… realize what I told you before… you are the wolf. The wolf only intensifies who you are… your anger, love, lust, everything is heightened, not just your senses, but your emotion… you laid down here for a reason."

Emily turned around, looking up at the sky and then back to see the apparition was gone. It was then she spotted it, the small outline of a dirt road, and she remembered where she had parked her truck two miles from the cabin. The wolf had brought her back to the truck, only on a different path. Emily moved through the wilderness. She knew it was cold; she could feel the frosted cold ground under her feet, but her skin burned still from the transformation. She broke out into the open to the truck and quickly opened the door. This wasn't the first time she had woken naked in the wilderness with no clothing; she pulled the seat forward, grabbing the bag. Quickly, she pulled the jogging outfit out. She promptly pulled a pair of pull-string pants up, followed by the sweatshirt over her head, Colin's sweatshirt. The extra pair of running shoes as she pulled them over her feet. She slammed the seat back as she jumped into the driver's seat and shut the door behind her. Her head fell to the steering wheel, and the horn blasted. She jumped back. She had let her anger do more than just get the best of her; it drove her to kill four men. She opened the ashtray, pulling the keys.

She had cried the entire way to her home. She half expected to see Don there, but the small driveway was empty, and she was happy. For the first time, she thought about her cell phone. She grabbed the bag from under the passenger seat, fiddling for a moment until she found it and checked it. Ten missed calls. She sighed. She looked. One was from Rosie, three from Meara, and it did not surprise her that the rest was from Don.

Emily jumped out of her truck and rushed up the drive and into the home. She didn't stop until she reached the bathroom, locking the door behind her and throwing her clothes into a hamper basket. She quickly jumped into the shower to get the blood and mud off her body. As she exited, she walked across the room, looking out the window where she sat down and looked outside. Tears began to fall as she looked at her phone, she slowly pushed the numbers in, and she knew them by heart even though the number wasn't saved on the phone. She had finished entering and then quickly deleted them as she laid her head on her arm, looking out the window.

The repeated knocks at her door woke her. Still sitting in the chair with her head resting on her arm, she saw him immediately, and he saw her. Don had a worried look on his face but also relief. Emily slowly stood, walking to the door. She quickly moved into his arms as the door spread. "I was worried about you," Don said.

"I'm sorry," she quickly replied.

"Are you okay?"

Emily pulled away, careful not to look him in the eyes. She wiped her face clear as she turned, walking into the house. Don was behind her, shutting the door.

"I will be," she lied. "When is the funeral, do you know?"

"The family wants a quick service. It'll be the day after tomorrow," he replied.

Emily paused, looking back. "Have they found him yet?"

"I've been listening to the scanner; the police are looking but believe he is held up somewhere with a friend of his. No one is talking, but you can be sure they will find him," he replied.

She knew they would. She knew they would find him and his friends savagely murdered by a wild animal. "I hope they do."

"I don't want you to be alone. He was here the other night… he may come back," Don replied.

"I can take care of myself." Emily forced a smile.

"I know you can," Don replied. "But I want to be here for you."

Emily returned to his side, hugging him and looking into his eyes. She smiled. "You already have been. More than you know." She gave him a peck on his lips. "But trust me… I can take care of myself." She pulled away, walking toward the back. She stopped leaning on the doorway. "I'm going to change and go to Rosie's. Do you want to go with me?"

"I have to work, but I will meet you there... I really wanted to make sure you were all right," he replied.

Emily looked at herself in the dresser mirror. She looked like she hadn't slept in days, and her face was flushed with tears. She barely knew Allison, but the woman was sweet and nice to her. She walked to her closet, opening it. There wasn't much clothing to choose from, not like her old closet. She grabbed the small dark blue skirt that would reach near the midway of her upper legs and a simple dark blue t-shirt that would reach as far as the skirt did down her body. She set down a purple scarf and a short sweater. She quickly undressed, finding simple dark underwear and putting them on, followed by dark tights and the skirt. She glared at herself in the mirror just before she put the shirt on, followed by the sweater. She grabbed Meara's dark brown boots from a few nights before and put them on. It was then she saw Don standing in the doorway. She forced a smile as she stood, grabbing the scarf from the bed. He smiled.

"You're simply beautiful."

"Shut up." She walked, giving him a kiss before walking past. She grabbed her cell phone from the table, knowing her bag was still in the truck from the night before. She shut the door behind them, sure to lock it as she went to her truck.

Chapter Sixteen

<hr>

A day had passed, and Emily had mostly avoided everyone in that time. She never got to attend Colin's funeral, and now she was planning on attending Allison's. Something about that felt wrong to her. She first needed a run to try and work off some excess anger. She had stopped her run; it was strange not going through the woods but the streets of Oakridge. She hadn't even realized she was this close to the police station. She wanted to avoid the woods, but especially other wolves. She had willingly killed four men; she had only wanted to kill the one. She did not want to be judged, though she was certain others knew, including Meara.

"Didn't realize you were a runner."

She was not surprised to see Kaylan once she realized where she was at. "Yeah, it's my release."

"You ever box?" the man questioned.

Emily rested her hands on her hips as she took a deep breath. It was obvious the deputy didn't know about his friends. "It would be stupid of me to put on boxing gloves with a guy I know doesn't like me."

"Sorry about the other day," Kaylan replied.

Emily sighed. She looked around. The man seemed sincere.

"I didn't…" He almost seemed sympathetic. "I didn't realize the extent of the abuse. I thought they were only having issues."

"And she's dead," Emily snapped. "And her child no longer has a mother." She felt the anger grow again. The same anger that allowed her to kill three men and feel nothing from doing it.

"I have no excuse." He stepped backward, holding the door open for her. "I promise to be gentle."

It was a promise Emily couldn't make. She took one more look around before entering the door. She had not seen much of the police station when she was there before, and she was surprised by the makeshift gym in the back. "Not a lot of people use it, but the gym is open to the public."

Emily tugged at her wet shirt, throwing it to the floor, revealing her sports bra. She picked up the gloves. They were heavier than she expected. Emily watched him bounce back and forth, throwing his gloves from side to side and loosening his arms. Emily held hers up, and as he stepped close, she jabbed. She put more strength into it than she should have. Kaylan reeled away, turning back and holding his jaw. She could tell he was forcing a smile. Nothing said as he stood and started bouncing around again. Emily let him circle, moving her feet to keep the man in front of her. Each jab connected perfectly with her gloves. He was taking it easy on her, not trying to hit her. She jabbed with her left, and a quick swing of her right arm again connected, reeling him in a circle away from her. It was then her phone went off, an alarm. "Are you going to Allison's funeral?"

Kaylan playfully twisted his jaw and let a half-smile grace his face. "Yeah." He looked at his watch.

"Will you drop me off at my place?" She had let time slip away from her.

Emily watched most of Allison's family pay their respects from a patch of trees on the edge of the cemetery. At the last minute she had changed her mind and decided not to be a part of the funeral services. She found herself almost hiding away watching from a distance. There were other wolves there. Alma was there, holding the cross around her neck gently. It made her think of Colin. Emily had wished she had gotten the chance to attend his funeral. To pay her respects. But also to make sure everyone there knew what an amazing friend and person he was.

"I am sorry for your loss." She knew Liam Bell's scent. He was close enough now she could almost taste it in the air around her.

"What do you want?" Emily questioned.

"It's a small town. It's a shame what happened to your friend. Nothing like that should happen to anyone. I wanted to pay my respects." There was a pause. "And see you."

Emily sighed as she looked around.

"Did you enjoy yourself the other night with the others?" Emily had stopped with her mouth standing wide open. He walked right up to her, not stopping until he was there at her side. "There are no secrets within the pack... especially when one of those you ran with was my flesh and blood." Liam smiled.

"I..." She wanted to run. Something she had realized; she had never seen Liam in his wolf form. Emily glanced in the direction of the funeral, and she could even see Alma glaring at her from the crowd.

"This isn't the place," she said turning to face him. She was surprised to see him in running gear, just as she was. She had planned on losing herself in the forest after the funeral and now he stood there in front of her giving her the opportunity.

"It is all right," he replied. "You have nothing to worry about."

Liam turned, walking away deeper into the forest, and though she hesitated, Emily followed. They walked the first few hundred feet but shortly after, he broke into a jog, and Emily sped up to keep pace. Then a sprint, Emily matched his speed, staying behind him but keeping the same distance between them. Then he broke out, feverishly running through the forest, and Emily's heart pounded as she rushed behind him. Faster and faster, they scurried through the wilderness with little worry for the approaching night.

Emily watched him stop as she came up to him. She couldn't fight the smile. The adrenaline pumped through her, her heart raced, and her legs enjoyed the rush. She enjoyed the no talking as it sent a thrill of excitement up her back. "A smile," Liam said, turning. He was as flushed as her. "I am happy to see you have a lovely smile."

"Maybe we got off on the wrong foot," Emily replied, standing straight as she caught her breath.

"No..."

Emily turned her head, puzzled at his response. "No?"

"I made a mistake... I was stalking your scent that night... the hunter was in the wrong place, and I lost control for a moment. It is all on me, how we met. How arrogant I came across. And your beauty when I saw you there that day, you radiate it." Emily smiled, lowering her head in embarrassment. "Blushing, another point in my favor."

Emily looked away and then up to the sky. As she looked back, Liam was again walking away from her further into the wilderness. "Most of my life… I've gotten everything I have ever wanted. The fast cars, the cheerleaders, on several occasions, I found myself on the wrong side of the law, and my father used his wealth to get me out of trouble." Emily rushed to catch up to him.

"So, you were a spoiled brat?" she questioned.

"Basically," he replied with a smile. "Have you ever let the wolf just run loose?"

"No," she quickly replied. "Not before the other night, anyways… not to the point I fed it my anger."

"I have never experienced any greater high," Liam replied.

"That's not me," she quickly replied, walking ahead when he stopped.

"I'll admit, I don't understand…" he replied, turning slowly, walking backward, and he rushed to catch up. "I understand the actions that turned you may not have been the best… but you'll learn most of all, werewolves have horrifying experiences regarding how they become the wolf. But it is who you are now. It won't be easy… especially at first, but the more familiar you get with that side of you, the more power you will have over it."

Emily smiled. She bit her lip as he turned away. She could smell the wolf in him. It radiated from every part of him, from how he talked to his walk and swagger. "Your daughter… you turned her?"

"No." He smiled. "My ex-wife did… much like you, she was attacked, unsure of what she was until it was too late. When she changed, she turned me and my daughter… my daughter was only five… she only knows the wolf, really."

"How long ago?" Emily rushed to catch up to his side.

"Sixteen years ago," he replied.

"And where is your ex-wife now?" Emily questioned.

"Out there somewhere." Liam seemed to motion off into the wilderness around them.

"So, you don't know?" Emily replied. She couldn't help but look at the lush undergrowth around them.

"No," he replied. Emily gauged his response, and she thought he was telling the truth. "I've hired private investigators… kept a watchful eye out for her, but nothing has turned up. I have lost faith she is even alive now. She's been gone nearly thirteen years now, she had a harder time controlling the wolf side of her. Or maybe she just got tired of me."

"Sorry," she replied.

"It was a long time ago," he replied. He jumped over a deadfall and turned to help her over. She could have easily climbed it as quickly and with as much ease as him but chose to let him help her. He grabbed her by the hips as she placed her hands down on his shoulders. She couldn't help but admire how strong his shoulders were and how tight his muscular hands gripped her hips as he slowly helped her down. Even holding her there freely in the air for a moment, he smiled. Emily blushed again. He released his grip and turned away. Emily grabbed his shoulder, turning him back to look at her. She ran her hand down his clean-cut face. He had a strong jaw and thin lips, his eyes a mysterious hazel. She slowly rose and kissed him as excitement ran through her body. When she was done, she walked past. "What was that for?" he questioned. She turned back, looking at him with an eager smile.

"For not being the guy I thought you were." She smiled.

"I am glad to prove you wrong." He smirked with a half-crooked smile she hadn't seen from him before. It was an extremely attractive smile, so much so that she forced herself to look away from him before he noticed.

"Where are we going?" She looked up to the sky. It would be dark in less than an hour.

"We can turn back if you want?" he replied.

"Or?" She turned, smiling. She stopped looking to the side, not sure where this was coming from. She was weak when he smiled. But when he didn't, the uneasiness was still there. But what she liked most now in the moment was that he knew what she was, and there were no worries about exposing her other side.

"There is an old logger's camp maybe a mile ahead," he replied, pointing off in the distance.

"That sounds interesting," she said.

They walked for a mile until they found an old cabin. Emily rushed forward and to the door. It was broken, barely hanging on its hinges. As he pushed it open, the squeal was loud.

"You said it was old," she said, turning and could not see Liam anywhere. She stepped back out, but he was gone.

She turned, walking into the old cabin. There was an old fire stove nearby. Axes and wood cutting tools hanging around the walls, all old and rusted. She smiled when she saw the bear trap lying in the corner; it was a one-room shack with no sign of anything resembling a bed.

"Rugged men lived here." She turned, holding her hand to her heart as Liam stepped inside. "Loggers, hunters, trappers, spend weeks at a time out here basically living off the wilderness."

"Yeah, sounds downright disturbing." Emily laughed.

"And on at least a few occasions, I've known wolves to stay out here when being part of humanity hasn't gotten too much for them. I have used it more than once since my wife turned my daughter and me." Liam looked away from her back to the door, and then he looked back at her again as he stepped into the cabin. "Those first three years were rough."

"When the two of you were turned, who helped you?" Emily questioned.

"A man known by Malcolm, he also introduced me to the pack though he is no longer a part of it… there were some differences of opinions between him and others," Liam added.

Emily turned to face Liam as he walked into the old cabin. He did not stop until he was close to her. He slowly raised his hand, placing it on her shoulder, but didn't stop until it rested on the back of her neck as he leaned in, pulling her closer to kiss. She felt her body drift into him instantly. Her hands went to his hips and the running pants. She could feel his erection through the thin cloth. She could feel his tongue push against her own for a moment, and then he bit down on her lip and pulled away. She had not even felt his hands as he pulled her short sleeve shirt up her body and over her head, tossing it to the musty floor. She didn't even try to resist as he pulled her bra down, exposing her nipples. He dragged his lips over them as she placed a hand on the back of his head. She moaned the moment she felt his teeth. She felt her other nipple being played with, with his hand. She looked down; his eyes were yellow, and his canines extended as he exposed his teeth.

"No," she muttered. The sight of his shifted eyes brought her back to reality. She couldn't do this. She couldn't let this happen with this man.

She felt her pants tug, pulling her body harshly. She cupped her hands around his face, forcing him to stand to her. Emily wanted to kiss him, to let him have her. It wasn't just the wolf. She wanted him.

He growled.

She returned the gesture.

"If you truly want me to stop…" He tried to pull away, her hands still tightly on his hips, holding him there against her.

"I don't know what I want." Emily wanted to cry. "I don't even know who the hell I am."

Emily felt his hands on her hips as he pried them away from his hips. "That is something you must find out for yourself. I've seen many try, but the Emily Meyer you want to be is no longer living inside you. You need to decide where it is you go from here. Who it is you can be and still live with yourself."

Emily wanted to smack him. Kiss him. She was as confused as ever about the man. The only thing she truly knew was he was dangerous. Then so was she and she was coming to embrace the realization daily.

"You will never be a wolf, not truly. Your heart is too pure. You need to figure out who you will be." He pulled away, his eyes still in intense anger and his canines enlarged as he placed his hands around her wrists pulling them away from his hips. "Don't take too long, Ms. Meyer." Just like that, he was gone, and for all her anger toward the man, she still wanted him.

Emily rushed through her house, leaving the front door open as she went straight into the bathroom. She dropped to her knees, just clearing the toilet as she retched. Over and over, she emptied her stomach into the toilet. She slowly sat beside it, leaning her head back onto the wall. "Fucking stupid," she muttered to herself.

Slowly she pulled herself up and began to strip until naked. She climbed into the shower and scrubbed until her skin blistered. As she stepped out, soaking wet, she jumped when she saw him.

"Some mistakes are meant to be made." Harrison grabbed the towel off a nearby rack and walked toward her. She noticed he kept eye contact with her the entire time, and she took the towel, wrapping it around her wet body. He turned, heading from the room.

"Give me a moment." He never turned back to look at her as she grabbed the robe, wrapped it around her body, and tied the string. She walked from the room out into the main living space. "I feel like the fucking head cheerleader, and everywhere I turn, I've got a football player dropping his pants and trying to impress me with the size of his dick, thinking I'll jump on it. Then I throw myself at one of y'all and I get rejected." She paused. "And you know… I'm not the only one who lives here. You all keep barging in. Eventually, Meara will be here."

"You were a runner in high school, track?" he questioned. "You won several bronze trophies in the 50 meters and 100 yards."

"Running was always a passion of mine," she replied. "You've been looking into my past?"

"I have…"

"You want me as just another pawn?" she questioned, taking a seat. "A play against Liam? Or should I say, Alma wants me as a pawn to use against Liam?"

"Liam has his habits… every few years, he pushes the buttons to see what he can get away with…"

"He is arrogant," she called out. "But he is also…"

"He is that, yes. And you can't blame yourself… our appetites are hard to contain sometimes," Harrison replied. "Liam is more in the public eye than I would like. He dabbles in back-room politics to further his wealth. He has, at times, garnered the attention of the media. But for his faults, he does a lot of good for our kind. He finances us, which allows us to seek out others like you, new to our world. He is not an evil man." Harrison ran a hand over his gray beard.

Emily lost all the air out of her as she slid down the couch. "I…"

"Liam has hunted people… when he was brought into the pack, he was wild as the wolf… he would stalk and kill. He never had complete control then. Enough control he had spaced out his killing, even knowing how to hide his tracks, yes, but I believe he felt guilt, but when you're young, it is so hard to control those impulses when you let the wolf run," Harrison replied.

"Why do you keep him in then? Why allow him to stay if he is a danger to people? He told me a person by the name of Malcolm brought him into the pack."

"Malcolm is still out there. He was… is… a dangerous man and stays mostly in upstate New York. There was bad blood from a lot of the older wolves in the pack back when Liam and his daughter were brought on. There are factions, some loyal to me, some to Liam, and even others with their own agendas, such as Olson and Chamberlain."

"Alma." Emily smiled.

"Alma is much stronger than she lets on, and she has the confidence and the morals to lead the pack," Harrison replied with a big smile of his own.

"How many are there… how many of us?" Emily questioned.

"Less than twenty in our pack, you've met most of us, but as far as we know, we are the biggest in the States… scattered from Oregon, through Canada, Alaska all the way down to New Mexico and California… Around the world… maybe 200, there is no way of truly knowing how many there are out there in the world. But here in the States, we barely break 60. There are others, of course. I am sure of it. Most people don't survive attacks. The percentage of people who survive is so small, 5 percent... Billions of people in the world, and there probably aren't a thousand werewolves among them. We are just a blip."

"How much of the world knows about us?"

Harrison smiled. "I don't know… I am certain there are government officials in dark shady rooms who know of our existence but must keep it to themselves. There are… contractors."

"Contractors…?"

"Hunters, people who know about us and hunt us." Harrison walked across the room. "They may consider us an abomination, blight on humanity, and try to hunt us into extinction." Emily showed no surprise at what he said. She had figured there were people out there in the world hunting her kind.

"If we are real… I know it sounds foolish, but what else is?"

"Not a foolish question in the least, and I am sure all of us have thought it one time or another. If werewolves are real… what else is out there? Like vampires, so often in fiction, there is a connection between the two entities… it is completely possible, I can't lie."

She couldn't hide her smirk as she looked down away from him. "I was raised a Christian, and it was so hard for me to even believe… the world I'm a part of now just seems so… impossible."

"Anything is possible… I have heard of doctors who know about us, who have tried to approach it as a disease, an infection, but have not been able to find a cure," Harrison replied. "There is a lot you don't know, or even a lot I don't know, and too much to unpack in an afternoon conversation. There are scholars out there who have studied, tracked history, and even written it in books. But that's another time and place to cover such things."

Emily looked down away before looking up at the much older man. "Why are you here?"

Harrison smiled; it was more of a smirk. "Not to further your regrets about coming here. We've not had any chance to talk one-on-one since your arrival, and I wanted if just for a moment to talk with you about what you are going to do from here."

"I don't know what I want," Emily replied. "Before the night I ran with the pack, I would have never seen myself letting the wolf run free like I did. And now, I don't know."

Harrison paused. He took a card from his pocket and then a pen writing a set of numbers on the back. "Alma, Morgan, and my numbers… don't be afraid to call if you need to talk."

"But there is something else," Emily said as she took the card. "Liam may not be the villain you believe him to be…. he rejected me tonight. Told me I needed to figure out what I wanted."

Harrison smiled, "I never believed Liam was the villain."

Chapter Seventeen

Emily hated the idea of taking the morning off work, but she traded shifts to get an afternoon shift. She drove two hours away from Oakridge before she found a place with Wi-Fi, and she felt comfortable enough to do it. She sat in a corner booth looking at the video browser. She called and hung up when the other person answered the phone, and it wasn't long before the person she wanted to see was online. She leaned forward, putting the earbuds in as the other person answered her call. Ashley's hair was chopped off, pixie short, and her eyes were lit with purple eye shadow and extended lashes. She was wearing a black overshirt.

"Bitch," was the first word out of her mouth when she saw Emily. Emily looked away to the side. "You know how long it has been since we talked? I've been worried sick about you. To figure out what you were going to do about the other wolves… And you look like shit."

"Thank you," Emily muttered. She could see her own camera. She didn't look like the same person she did a few months before. She wasn't the same person. "How is Mom?" Emily questioned. Ashley looked away. There was someone else in the room with her, then back to the camera. "Ashley, how are they?"

"As good as to be expected when their only child disappears," Ashley said. "Your dad, he works a lot. I don't see him, thankfully. Your mom says it is nothing… but I think he sleeps at his office often. And she has been staying at your old grandmother's house in Williamson…"

"Why is she staying there?" Emily questioned. It didn't surprise her to hear that her father was hardly around. Even when she was home, he was hardly ever at home. But for her mom to be staying at her deceased grandmother's house, sent a chill over her.

"I hear from her daily, and she asks me if I have heard from you each day." Ashley gritted her teeth. "You should call and talk to her. She knows I'm lying about knowing where you are. She just hasn't called me out on it."

"I wish I could come home." Emily wiped at her eyes. She was on the edge of tears. It was the first time she had voiced it, but now that she did, it was all that she was honestly thinking about. She wanted to go home.

"I see Detective Hastings once a week. He has been looking for you, and I think he has me under surveillance, even has my phones bugged…"

"Where are you now?"

"At a friend's house," she replied. "There is no open investigation. No one beside him is looking for you… all those deaths were ruled animal attacks… they found a wolf, dead, I don't know if it was one like you or what… or why it didn't shift back to human, so it must have been a real… someone had to plant it to cover for you. Lauren, maybe?"

"No…" Emily thought about Harrison. It was something he would do.

"How…" Ashley paused, and Emily could tell she was trying to figure out what she was going to ask.

"How am I dealing with that other part of me?" She could see Ashley nod. "I… I went for a run with the other wolves… a couple, actually… I almost hate to admit I enjoyed it."

"Fuck…" Ashley paused.

"I know I shouldn't say that, but it was natural." Emily laughed. Nothing about the situation she found herself in was natural.

"What do they want with you?"

"They want me to join them and become part of their pack," Emily said.

"What are you going to do?"

"The run… it was…" Emily replied.

"How did that feel?" Ashley questioned.

"Like… like I was being reborn, for the first time since the attack, I felt right," Emily replied.

"Do you have control?"

"I had control with them…" Emily sat back in her seat, looking around the small restaurant. There were only two other people there. "It felt natural to me, but…"

"But you still felt guilty afterward, always hard on yourself if you allowed yourself to have anything resembling fun." Ashley smirked. "What are you going to do? Are you going to join them?" Emily looked away as if she was deep in thought. "Whatever you choose, as long as you don't go so long without contacting me. You look like skin and bones, like you haven't been getting enough food in you or enough sleep." Ashley again looked away from the camera and back.

"You should call your mother. Video call her on this. I'll make sure she gets my laptop tomorrow."

"I don't sleep," Emily replied with a smirk. "And thanks, what a girl always wants to hear, she looks like shit."

"I didn't say that the new hair isn't nice." Ashley smiled. "It's not the fiery red I remember, and I can't believe you cut it."

"I knew people would be looking for me," she replied. "I think I need to go."

Ashley frowned.

"I promise I'll keep in touch."

"Emily, be safe." Ashley blew a kiss toward the camera. Emily could tell her friend was forcing her smile and on the edge of tears because she was as well. "Emily, if it helps… I think you can come home. Hastings has nothing… there is no one else looking for you. There are no open investigations. I have a friend who investigated that for us… you are free to come home. I love you."

"I love you too, Ashley."

The drive back to Oakridge seemed to take forever. Emily was lost in her thoughts the entire way back and on the edge of tears. She was a little early when she came into the diner. She stood at the back door, trying to force one last long drag off the cigarette. She needed to quit; she knew that. She wondered how the smoking affected the wolf.

Chloe stepped into the back room. "There is a guy here wanting to speak to you."

Emily smiled, thinking of Don. She walked past the other woman into the main diner. She wanted to retreat when she saw Madison standing at the counter. "You've been summoned." He scooted off the stool and walked toward the door, stopping before stepping out to ensure she was following.

Emily wanted to make a scene, she wanted to say fuck you and go back into the back, but she followed him out the door, down the street, into the clerk's office. "What the fuck? I'm not someone you can just summon like a pet, you bastard."

"Forgive Madison. He sometimes can forget how to act." Liam was dressed in a long green jacket.

"Around cattle," Emily growled.

"I'm sorry, I should have come myself…"

"Instead, you sent your mutt." Emily snarled at him.

"Again, I apologize,"

She turned to look at Liam, and he nodded at Madison. Madison started walking toward the door. "Like a good little bitch, obey." Emily's emotions were running high. She was thinking about her friends and family. This was a surprise she didn't need or want.

"I wanted to see you again." He approached, circling around behind her. He shifted her hair away from her neck, and a chill went up her body as he kissed her where her shoulder and neck met. "I missed you. I miss your smell." He kissed her neck again; she felt his hands on her hips, pulling him back against him, and feeling his hard body against her brought her back to reality.

"This can't happen." She pulled out of his grip, turning to face him. "The other night… it was a mistake, Liam… You rejected me. Some part of you knows I need more time. More time than you've given me."

He raised his head in a questioning glare. "What's wrong?"

"Everything," she replied. "The other night, I let the wolf, I let it control me…"

Emily wasn't talking about the evening she had spent with Liam, and she could see the confusion growing on his face. "What are you trying to say?"

"I just need more time. You did the right thing the other night… I would have let you have me if you'd stayed, but you didn't, and I'm thankful for that," she replied.

"Okay," Liam said with a nod as he looked away from her for a moment. "I've got to go out of town for a few weeks…"

Emily watched as the man bit down on his lower lip, and it sent a chill of excitement over her forcing her to turn away. "I'll be here when you get back, and we can talk then."

"I'm going to hold you to that," Liam said, almost with a bow, before he turned and walked away from her.

Emily entered the diner and quickly found a place to sit. There were two of the older women waiting tables, Irene and Patricia. Emily wasn't familiar with either. She set her head down on the table and closed her eyes.

"You must have had an eventful night." She looked up to see Alma standing up at the edge of the table beside her. She was dressed in loose-fitted dark pants of loose material, a simple thin dark-colored shirt, and a mixed tan-colored scarf. Her skin was dark and flawless, her hair wild, and Emily would not lie; she was happy to see her. She sat across from her.

She leaned forward, pulling the menu closer. "I'm here because I knew Allison, and I know you. It's a small town."

"I'm sorry," Emily replied, sitting up and looking out the window. She took a long deep breath and slowly exhaled it.

"Controlled breathing. Your hand has a touch of a shake." Alma leaned forward as Emily looked. She watched the woman place her hand with her purple fingernails on her hand. "You need some caffeine. Something to calm your nerves." She waved at the nearest waitress. "Two of your strongest coffees, please." The waitress, Patricia, a sixty-something woman with graying hair, gave Emily a quick glance before she walked away. "I can smell them on you." Emily looked at her; the woman's dark eyes changed to an intense yellow. Emily didn't have to elaborate any further. Alma's face curved into a smile. Emily could smell death on the other woman and the familiar scent of the men she had killed days before.

Emily bit her lower lip as she looked around. "Am I to be punished or something…"

"No, the others, they don't know, just me and Bethany," Alma replied.

"Why?"

"A woman is beaten to death by her abusive boyfriend…" Alma smiled. "We were going, hunting them to do the same as you. It's our secret, that I promise you. There is the pack… and then there is the sisterhood among the pack. Every male within is vying to be the alpha, lead the others, and be in charge, which often leads to heads butting. Rarely do women lead the pack, but we are united as sisters."

"I didn't go there to…"

"Yes, you did," Alma replied, watching as the waitress sat the two coffees down.

Emily frowned. The other woman was right, and Emily had no excuse but to let her grief and anger take control of her. "She was a good person… I only knew her for a brief time, but she was good. She didn't deserve this."

"Often, people don't get what they deserve, and more often than not, the innocent and the best of us are the ones who are hurt for no other reason than they are good souls," Alma unwrapped her scarf, placing it beside her.

"You believe in a higher presence?" Emily questioned.

"Do I believe in God? Yes," Alma said, placing her hand on the wooden cross still around her neck. "I believe in Heaven and Hell, and the things we do in this life influence us after lives. I believe prayer works but only in lifting one's spirits. Sometimes we need help."

"And you believe God allowed this to happen to us, to be cursed?" Emily asked.

"You see it as a curse. Some of us see it as a gift." The woman smiled. Her smile was bright and full of confidence in who she was and what she believed in. Her lips were full and with purple color insinuating their beauty.

"How can it be a gift, what we are?" Emily questioned.

"We have the power to do things others can't," she replied. "And with practice and patience, we have control of the other self."

"Sounds like I'm disturbing a deep conversation," Meara said as she sat down beside Alma. Don sat down beside Emily. She was glad to see both. Don's hand found its way between them to hers, and she felt her chest burn as they intertwined.

Alma smiled as she looked at Emily. "Happy couple." Emily could feel her temperature rise and her natural paleness as she blushed.

"We're not..." Don looked at Emily, and she finally looked at him, and she could see it in his eyes. "Are we?"

"We haven't talked about it," Emily replied.

"You are. Just how the two of you just reacted, you are," Meara replied with a mischievous grin on her face. Emily felt bad. She liked Don. She was conflicted about Liam but no longer hated him like she once did. There was an attraction to Liam she couldn't deny, she would want to blame it on the wolf side of her, but even she knew it would be a lie. She passed a glance to Alma, and she could feel her blush deepen as the other woman smiled. The wolf liked Alma and that was an entirely different situation.

It was at this time the bells went off, catching their attention. Emily turned just as three men entered the diner, all in police uniforms. Emily recognized them as two of the town's four deputies and Sheriff Bell. They stepped up to the counter, and the sheriff looked in their direction and he instantly started toward them. "Don," he said with a nod. "Sarah, would you care if I talked to you privately?" Emily frowned.

"Sure," she replied. Don exited, allowing Emily out of the booth, and she followed the sheriff outside.

She turned as the sheriff walked out the door behind her. She saw Don and the two deputies shortly after that. The sheriff circled around her, and she instantly felt Don's arms wrapped around her. She shivered as she looked back, trying to smile, but it was forced. As their eyes met, he hugged tighter, and she looked back to the sheriff. Bell's uniform was loosely fitted with his big dark sunglasses on his bald head like she remembered him from before, but his goatee was thicker and more unruly. He smiled, looking at the two of them. "Eugene was last seen at your place, Sarah… he threatened you once before… I'd like to leave a deputy watching over you while we search for him."

"…That won't be necessary," Emily replied. She tried to think of a reason, but it did not occur to her at the time.

"It won't be necessary, Sheriff. I can keep an eye on her while you are searching for him." The sheriff gave her an odd look and then looked at Don. It was at this time Alma stepped out of the diner as well.

"I will be staying with her as well, Sheriff," Meara said, following her out the door.

"I will be all right," Emily quickly spoke up. She was uneasy; she did not like all the attention she was getting.

"I don't care who stays with her, as long as someone stays with her until Eugene is found." The sheriff nodded as he turned to walk away with the two deputies on his heels.

"They'll find him and put him away for what he did to Allison," Meara said, giving Emily a knowing glare.

"Yes, they will," Alma peeped in.

Emily was the first in the door. Though the sheriff had said he wouldn't place a deputy on her, she immediately noticed the car that had followed her and the others back to her place. She knew it was Kaylan. She could smell his aftershave. She went as far as to wave as she shut the door behind her. She turned, taking a deep breath and looking at Don, Alma, and Meara.

"You know you all don't have to stay here, well…" She looked at Don. "You can stay. But you don't have to stay, Alma."

Meara took off her overshirt and placed it on the couch, revealing her white tank top and black bra. Emily watched Alma and smirked. The woman was checking her out. "They can both stay."

"I think I'll stay too," Alma said. "Tell me you have any food." The woman turned to look at them as she stepped into the kitchen." She opened the fridge. "You have a grill outback?"

"Yeah," Emily replied. The woman was taking over. She looked directly at Emily. It was as if she wanted to get her alone to finish the conversation from earlier.

"I'll start it up," Don replied, walking toward the back door and out.

Meara disappeared into the bathroom, and Emily moved quickly to Alma's side. "Your tattooed friend is cute," she replied, "But I can smell Liam all over her. I assume you do as well."

"What do you want?" Emily questioned. "Meara's not sleeping with Liam…" Emily wondered if it had gone unnoticed by the other woman. Emily had to also smell of Liam and Madison.

"You, alone for ten minutes," she replied. Emily blushed again as she felt her heart race and she could see Alma smirk in response.

The door from the outside opened, and Don stepped back inside. "Grill is started. I went ahead and started a fire in the pit as well." He walked on past, getting a good look out the window. "Deputy is still there."

Alma walked past toward the back and out into the back-porch area. Emily walked until she was in the bedroom by herself. She sat on the bed and took a deep breath as she pulled the scarf out from around her neck, letting it lie on the bed. Next came the sweater, it was uncomfortable, and she needed to breathe. She lay back on her bed, closing her eyes.

"What are you thinking?" She heard his voice, followed by the sound of the door shutting behind him.

"Nothing," she replied.

"Liar," he replied. She could feel him getting closer as all the hairs on her body tingled.

She was lying. "What do you think I'm thinking?" She smirked but did not open her eyes. She could feel him there, close enough to touch, but he didn't.

"You're thinking, if only you had done something the other night when he was here… Allison would still be alive," he replied.

She opened her eyes, rising just a little bit on her elbows. "Yeah, so what if it is true?"

Don placed his arms on her legs, looking up at her. "What could you have done?"

Killed him, she wanted to say. "I don't know," she replied.

"It could have been you and not Allison, or maybe the both of you," he replied.

She sat up, running her hands through his shaggy hair and down through his beard with a smile. She set her head down on his forehead and took a deep breath. She felt his hands make their way around her.

"I've lost…" There was a pause as she twisted her head to the side. "I've lost a lot in a noticeably brief time in my life. A lot changed, but I am still unsure how to move forward. I wish things were different. I wish I could go back to the boring life I lived before. But I can't. And I have a tough time trusting other…" There was another long pause as she rose to make sure he was looking at her in the eyes. "I'm not sure if I trust you. You're just here when I think I need someone the most. Like an angel." She smiled again, running her hand down the side of his face.

"I'm no angel," Don replied. He rose to kiss her, and she placed a hand between them, resting on his chest. "We all have a past; some of us run from it. Some of us can, but some of us can't. And we all have to accept that."

"You're not even real," she said, kissing him. She stood, pushing him away to his feet and putting some space between them. She approached her closet, grabbed a sweatshirt from it, and turned to see him standing. "Let's go join the others."

They walked out, but Alma and Meara were nowhere to be seen. They found them in the backyard near the fire pit, sitting quite close to one another. "Don't the two of you look comfortable," Don said, grabbing two beers and handing one to Emily.

"Had to find some way to entertain ourselves. The only man candy was inside," Alma said with a smile.

"Eww, that's my father," Meara quickly pointed out.

Alma smiled. "We were talking faith."

"Oh no, has she been trying to convert you?" Don questioned.

"To Pagan?" Alma said with a smile showing her cross. "There isn't a chance of that. But we agree on quite a few philosophical views of life. How the world would be a better place if people loved and respected all no matter their beliefs, sexual orientation, race, or gender."

"I thought I saw light back here." The deputy appeared with his flashlight and gun drawn.

"Now we have some more man candy." Alma smiled and winked at the deputy before she took a drink of the beer. Instantly, the young deputy seemed to blush, and every one of them laughed except Emily whose eyes met Alma's, she was jealous of how open the other woman was flirting or maybe she was just jealous of the attention she was getting.

"Want a beer, Officer Kaylan?" Meara questioned.

"Sorry, on duty," Kaylan replied, looking straight at Emily.

"We won't tell if you don't," Alma replied.

"I just wanted to give you an update. They found Eugene's vehicle and several others, but not them. They took a mountain road into the wilderness, and they could be anywhere," the deputy said.

Emily's eyes grew wide as she glared at Alma, and she winked and smiled, taking another drink of her beer. She had a feeling she knew now why the woman wanted to talk to her so badly. "What does that mean, Officer?" She looked back to the deputy.

"It means you probably have nothing to fear from him," he replied.

"That means I can have my house to myself." She smiled.

"Are you trying to kick us out?" Alma questioned.

"I would like to get some sleep."

"I'm not letting you stay here alone," Don replied.

"I still live here," Meara spoke up so everyone would notice she was still there.

"I'll still be parked out until the sheriff tells me to leave," the deputy said with a smile.

"And I'm still staying the night," Alma spoke up.

Emily sighed.

Half the night passed, and she slipped out of bed, leaving Don there asleep as she stepped out into the main room. She had left Alma and Meara on the couch when they went to bed; she half expected to see neither, but Alma lay there, watching her. "What the hell?"

"Don't you mean where the hell?" Emily rushed across the living room to join her.

"Where the hell are they?"

"Some place far enough away they aren't likely to be discovered until the snows thaw in the spring," she replied with a smile. "And your shredded clothing is in the trunk of my car."

Emily took a deep breath. "Thank you."

"Do you trust Meara?" Alma questioned.

Emily took a deep breath. "I'm safe with them."

"Meara is becoming too close to the pack... her constant involvement with pack bonfires, her friendship with you, and now her flirtation with Liam or even your flirtation with him," her voice dropped to no more than a whisper.

"No..." Emily paused, looking to the door with a gaping mouth.

"Some members of the pack have a wilder streak than others. Madison, Chamberlain, and Julianne... they can be dangerous. They play at life as if they are better than others within the pack, but especially better than normal people. And

Liam doesn't have the control over them he thinks he does. You need to watch over your friend then, don't let her get caught in the middle of what may come down between the two of you…

"They will see Meara as a bargaining chip…"

"And Don?"

"As a threat," Alma said.

Emily looked back at her own closed door to the room, and she growled as she turned back to Alma who only smiled.

Chapter Eighteen

Emily woke. The last thing she remembered was sitting next to Alma on the couch. She rolled over; the other woman must have helped her into her bed during the night. She slowly got up, still wearing the sweatpants and sweatshirt. She slowly crossed into the living room but saw no one.

She saw the note taped to the door. "Will be in touch – Alma."

She smiled as she slowly opened the door, and the police car was gone as well. She took a deep breath and sighed relief, happy to be alone again. It was too late for her to retreat when she saw Andrea. "I am so glad I caught you home." The perky woman walked up to her with a big smile. "Is Meara home?"

"No," Emily replied.

"Too bad, we're having a little get together up the road, it would be nice if you came by," the woman said.

"I'll think about it," Emily said as she looked in the direction of her neighbor's house.

She shut the door returning to the bedroom, quickly pulling the sweatpants off, followed by the rest of her clothing as she headed to the shower.

Despite Emily's better judgment, she did go to the neighbor's, Emily smiled, watching Andrea and her husband. It was surreal; Andrea annoyed her with her consistent nosiness. She was happy seeing some normalcy in the two of them. They were living the perfect marriage right down to the white picket fence. She continued smiling as she watched Andrea approach with a bottle of beer. "I am so glad you could make it," Emily replied with a smile of her own. She was amazed at how big the other woman's smile always seemed to be.

"Thank you for the invite." Emily took a big drink of her beer.

"Mingle, have fun, don't be shy." Andrea ran a hand down Emily's arm before she turned and walked away. Emily took another big drink, still smiling at the normalcy. It had been months since she had found herself in a situation that was anything close to normal. There were at least fifteen people at the barbeque, and she recognized most from the diner, even if she could not always put names to faces.

She saw him then, and her own reality came crashing down around her. She was not sure how she missed him. Madison was a head taller than everyone else at the event. His smile stretched across his face as he approached, taking a seat beside her. "What are you doing here?"

Madison took a drink of his own beer before replying, "Keeping an eye on you."

"Why?" Emily quickly replied.

Madison's grin grew impossibly bigger and caused her stomach to churn. "Liam sees potential in you."

"I want nothing to do with Liam. He and I have an understanding. He is going to give me some space until I get some things figured out," Emily said.

"You assume you have a choice." Madison downed his beer and tossed the bottle into the fence, busting it. "Liam's out of town… and maybe I'll take my turn to try an break you."

"She does." Emily turned to see Alma stepping up. Emily quickly looked back at Madison, and she could see the frustration on his face. "What is Liam's game? What is he playing at?" Emily thought about the first meeting with them and how Madison had slapped her.

"Liam's out of town, he told me himself." Emily looked to Alma, who seemed to be ignoring that part of the conversation.

"You shouldn't be here, little girl," Madison growled.

"The games are going to end. The playing with people's lives, they are going to end now before they start," Alma replied with a growl of her own. Emily could see the anger in the other woman's face; her peaceful light tan eyes changed red and yellow. The woman could change now. She was so angry. Emily looked; no one else had noticed the intense conversation.

"We need to leave." Emily stood, not looking back at Madison.

"You are out of line, little girl," Madison said. She could hear the man as he stood and felt him hover over her.

"Not here and not now." Emily placed her hand on Alma's jaw, making the woman look in her eyes. "There are people here. Innocent people."

It had started to grow dark as they approached Emily's home. Alma panted. Emily could feel her skin was boiling hot. "He is gone."

"I am sorry," Alma said.

"Times are changing." Alma bolted to her feet as Madison seemed to appear out of the darkness.

Emily backed away until she was several steps behind Alma. "I want you to leave. You're not welcome here." She could see his eyes, yellow and full of hate and anger. She knew he was on the edge of a transformation.

"Don't," Alma said in a harsh tone. Emily could see the other woman remove her layered bracelets, letting them fall to the ground, followed closely by her cross.

"Stop me," Madison growled as he removed his shirt.

Emily stepped backward, seeing Alma remove her dress and toss it to the ground without hesitation. Emily was shocked at the sight of the other woman's body. Her back, legs, and shoulders were ripped as she could see every muscle in the woman's body. She had seen her naked before but did not see the details of her frame until now. "I will kill you, Madison."

"You will try and die for it, little girl this has been a long time coming, bitch."

Emily quickly removed her shirt and watched as Madison began to turn. Alma glanced back at her. "Stay out of this. This is my fight, pack politics, and I don't want or need your help. I'm here to keep you out of this. To give you the option you deserve." She pushed her panties down her legs before she dropped to her knees, beginning her own change.

Emily watched them. She unbuttoned her pants and kicked off her shoes despite what Alma had said to her. She knew she needed to be ready to shift. She could not let Madison live. She could feel her own wolf wanting out, wanting to protect Alma. Her eyes met Alma's. The peacefulness was gone. Now the other woman's eyes looked much like Madison's, full of anger and intended violence.

Madison was fully turned. The look in his eyes as he glared past Alma and at her eyes sent a chill up her back. Emily was thankful he seemed to wait at least until the other wolf was completely out. She watched him snarl. The sheer size of him made her heart race with fear. He was large as a human, and the only way she knew how to describe him now was monstrous. Brown fur seemed to shine in the waning light. It would be completely dark soon. Alma stood tall still between them; her fur was light brown and streaked with dark curls matching her more natural hair. She looked back to Emily as she snarled, eyes distinctive to the woman she had come to respect and care for in a short amount of time.

Madison approached, snarling before he released a roaring growl meant for intimidation, but Alma only stepped forward. The hair on the back of Emily's neck stood, and her stomach heaved as she dropped to her knees. She looked up as she cleared her mouth to see Alma leap.

Emily felt the tension in her own body continue to grow. She could feel it in the old wound on her side, and she screamed, "No, no, no!" She glanced up to see Alma being thrown away from Madison. He looked at her before the other wolf, approaching with a gaping mouth full of saliva and a thirst for blood. Madison had size over Alma, and it was the only advantage he needed. Emily knew the outcome of the fight, seeing how easily he had tossed the smaller wolf aside. He was going to kill Alma. Emily's wolf would not allow it.

Emily had regained her composure enough to see what was happening. Madison towered over Alma, and her heart raced. She sprung to her feet just as Madison lifted the smallest of the three wolves from the ground. She heard Alma growl, and then the sound of pain as Madison's massive jaws latched onto her shoulder.

Emily attacked. Feverishly, she dug her claws into the largest wolf's back, but Madison did not release. He shook violently. Emily latched onto his arm; she could feel his muscles tense under her bite, but still, he shook so violently that Emily could smell the warm scent of Alma's blood. Even felt it as it splashed from Madison's jaws to Emily's face.

He shook until Emily could no longer hold her grip, and she fell off. He watched him toss Alma and turn toward her. She could see his smile through the crimson-stained jaws and lips as fresh plasmas and slobber dripped to his massive chest. He howled. It was a confident howl followed by a laugh, never slowing his progress as he stood over top of her. He leaned to swipe his massive claws at her. As he did, he lunged forward violently. Alma was on his back, slashing and clawing.

Emily rushed to her feet and charged. She reached them just as Madison pushed Alma away. Now Emily clawed at the freshly opened wounds, opening them wider. He tossed her away like he was flicking a flea. He was wounded now; she could taste his blood on her tongue. Emily did not wait; she rushed him again and saw Alma doing the same. He released a roar as two sets of teeth dug into flesh. He slashed and shook wildly, attempting to get them off him. Emily fell first, right below him. She could see Alma's claws as they dug into his rib cage, each cut going deeper causing blood to splatter on the ground. She saw Madison's eyes, filled with terror, and she growled. He knew he was going to die. He grabbed and pushed Alma off him and whirled to run. Emily leaped. Onto his back, she bit into the side of his neck. He reached and snatched at her but missed both times. She felt the violent forward motion, not realizing it was Alma hitting him low and knocking him to the ground. Emily rolled away and back to her feet to see Alma dig further into the man's back, but he never moved. They had killed him.

Emily fell to her back, exhausted; she felt the growing sensation as she was changing. She had lain there only ten minutes, but it had felt like longer. She ached. She was scratched in several places, but nothing major. Or so she thought. She felt too weak to check for herself. She rolled over to see Madison's limp nude body and smiled. Part of her hated herself for smiling. She had helped kill a man. But still, she smiled. She did not want to kill him, but he had left little choice. "Alma?"

She could not see the other woman but knew she had suffered several bad wounds. "Alma?" She rushed to her feet; the other woman was just on the other side of Madison. Back to her petite, muscular human form. Emily rushed to her, her eyes open, looking up at her. "You need a doctor."

"I will heal."

"Emily looked at the bite wound on her shoulder. "You're really badly hurt… your shoulder." Blood continued to pour from the wound, and Emily fought to hide the urge to throw up, still tasting Madison's blood in her throat.

"We have to get rid of the body." Emily looked around, the fight had taken them to the forest line, and the lake was not far away.

When Emily opened the door, Morgan rushed through the home; he did not stop until he was beside Alma. "Is he dead?" he looked up at Emily, still covered in blood and dirt.

"Yes," she replied without hesitation.

"Good," Morgan replied. He whipped the hair out of Alma's face.

"I didn't know what else to do," Emily replied.

Morgan turned to look at her. "Come." He got up, rushing out to the back; he didn't stop until standing over his pack member's body. "You are fucking bastard, always causing trouble." Morgan looked around. Emily watched as he ran and grabbed a tarp and quickly carried it over to the body and wrapped it up. He picked it up, carrying it to his own car and putting his massive body in the trunk.

"What are you going to do with him?" she questioned, and he looked at her.

"Do you really want to know?"

"No…"

"Watch over her. I'll come back for her," he said as he got into his car and drove away.

Chapter Nineteen

"Damn it."

Emily's skin continued to itch and crawl. She dug the rough scratcher into the palm of her hand, back and forth, with fierce intentions.

"It is in your mind." Emily turned to see Alma standing in the doorway of the kitchen. She wore a t-shirt two sizes too big for her slender frame.

"What?" Emily turned, running the hot water over her hands.

"The blood," Alma replied. "You have to let go of it, or you will always see the blood on your hands." Alma crossed the room to Emily's side, and she could feel the other woman's cold hands on her wrists as she fought at the tears. Emily never wanted the blood to go away, to forget what she had become or done. "But it amuses me that you seem to be having such a tough time dealing with killing Madison as you did those bastard rednecks."

"How long have you been a wolf?" Emily took a deep breath looking at the other woman in the mirror.

"A long time," Alma replied, pulling Emily's hands away from the scalding water.

"How did you last so long without…"

"Without going crazy?" Alma smiled. "Who said I haven't?" Alma pulled her away from the sink and into the living area, not stopping until the two women were on the couch, and Emily could feel her as the other woman forced her to take a seat. "The loneliness… it was brutal, I won't lie. I always enjoyed being alone, being different before… After, I found I didn't like it so much."

"How did it happen… the attack?"

"I was nineteen, my last few months of high school… I was a bit of a wild child." Emily watched her smile. It was her eyes. Emily had no problem seeing this woman having a wilder streak than the motherly feeling she radiated now. "While most of my classmates were into sports, showing their school spirit, drag racing and getting drunk on a Saturday night and being good little Christian angels on Sunday mornings, I was painting, drawing, sneaking into cemeteries, taking photographs on the full moon."

Emily had a feeling she knew where the story was going. "That is where I saw him for the first time. Age didn't matter to me, he was older, and well, he was wild. His sleek blue eyes were like liquid, and he had short, perfect brown hair and a perfect scuffed beard; he looked like he'd stepped off a movie screen. I snapped his photograph without him knowing." Emily could see Alma almost blushed at the thought of him. "The first time we kissed, I was the aggressor… sort of, I backed him into this corner where he had no choice but to kiss me, and it was every bit as amazing as I had imagined."

Emily smiled. "The wolf."

"He fucked like an animal, raw, wild, uncontrollable, and completely insatiable. The things we did…"

Emily knew she was older, but still looked several years younger. "How did he turn you?"

"I had plans, was going to go away for school, and I knew we wouldn't last as a couple. I intended on breaking it off before I left. It was the week of prom. We went to a secluded spot, watched the sun set, and just lay together in the moonlight. I almost felt guilty for what I was going to do to him. I never got the chance. He was so strong; I had never realized how much so before that night, how strong he was for a thin frame. I was scared… That was before the eyes. His once sleek, seductive blue eyes changed to something yellow and feral. I sat there watching him change, unable to run away. I couldn't even scream for help, even though it wouldn't have done me any good. I just sat there in horror and shock as a man I had been sleeping with became a demon before my eyes. His breath as he snarled, looking down on me… He latched onto my shoulder and shook." Alma pulled the shirt down off her shoulder, and Emily could see the scars. She thought of her own, where Devon had latched onto her side, and the small red marks were still there, and at times, she could still feel the old wound. Especially when she turned. "For weeks after that, he kept me locked away, nursed my wounds, but never spoke to me. The seizures started, and I just wanted to die. He kept me locked away, and I had no idea what was happening to me until the first transformation." Alma smiled, even laughing for a moment.

"What?" Emily questioned, confused.

"He was a fool. He never turned… he stood there with a smug look on his face, those muscular arms spread across his chest, and just watched. Watching what he had done to me…"

"You killed him…"

"The moment I was on my feet, he had wanted me for his mate, I could remember him saying. Even through the pain, I remember him saying I was his forever. It wasn't until after that did I rediscover my faith."

"What will they do to us?" Emily questioned, "The others in the pack?"

"Madison was a nut case… it was only a matter of time before he exposed us, and no one will do a thing to you or me… I promise you this," Alma replied.

Emily sighed. She wanted to be punished. She'd killed a man. Again. Her stomach churned as she felt sick. She rushed to the bathroom closing the door behind her as she hurled.

Emily went straight from home to the church. "Forgive me, Father, for I have sinned."

Emily lowered her head, thinking about her life. Her thoughts were all over the place: Colin, Liam, Ashley, Meara and Don, her parents, and even Alma. She was torn with lust, feeling lost. With the taste of her own blood on her lip, she wanted to hunt now more than ever before. The freedom of running with other wolves was bliss. For the first time ever, she was happy with her condition.

"I'm having a crisis of faith." Emily took a long deep breath.

She loved the beauty of the old church; the state of decay gave it a new life. She saw them all there in that moment. Everyone who had an influence on her, her grandmother, who was always there to pick her up when her parents were fighting, when she only wanted to escape the loud noises coming from downstairs, she'd run to her. Her mom, whenever her father would get mad at her for not having quite the test scores, he had wanted her too. Ashley, who was always there when she needed that shoulder to lean on. All watching over her.

"I never understood this." Emily turned. Julianne, her arms extended so she could hit both rows of chairs in the aisles. "How man could put so much faith in a fairy tale When we walk amongst them and they don't even know it."

"What do you want?" Emily questioned, turning away from Julianne. She took a deep breath letting her head fall back. She wanted to be left alone. Left alone with her thoughts and her depression, as she desperately wanted to find a place in this world.

"Who do you think you are?" she questioned, circling around until she entered the row in front of Emily.

"What?" Emily questioned, getting up off her knees and taking a seat.

"Who do you think you are to refuse my father's advances? You think you are better than him?" she questioned. Emily just shook her head. "You act like you're better than the rest of us, but you're nothing but a pup, a bitch that needs to learn her place."

"Where is my place?" Emily questioned. "As your father's plaything?"

"If that is what he wants, you should see it as a pleasure."

Emily laughed. She started to stand, but the other woman leaped over, knocking her back into the chair.

"I don't take kindly to someone laughing at me." The younger woman was stronger than she seemed, pinning

Emily. She tried to move, but her position kept Emily from moving.

"Be serious, little girl," Emily growled.

Julianne lowered her head, replying with a growl of her own. "I'm serious." She slashed, cutting into Emily's cheek. Blood dripped from Emily's face, she started to stand, but the other woman pushed her weight into her, stopping her from budging. Emily felt a panic attack coming along. Her heart raced, and her breathing became ragged. Julianne began to laugh. "You're not so tough. You killed Madison, you and that bitch, Alma… We still haven't found Alma, but I am sure when the others do, she will die a miserable death at their hands."

"Who?" Emily tried to fight, moving away from her position.

"Others in the pack, others who are loyal to my father. Harrison, Alma, your little bitch boy Morgan will all die horrible little deaths, and this pack with be his… then you will have no other option. You will be his little plaything for as long as he deems it. Until someone else comes along, and you will be happy just to have your throat still attached." Julianne smiled.

She reached forward, wiping blood from Emily's face. She smiled as she stuck her tongue and slowly licked her finger clean. "My, you're sweet." Emily took a deep breath and pushed herself up by her legs. She pushed the woman off into the row of seats away from her. Emily turned and started up the aisle. She was about to start running when she came to a stop. Julianne jerked her back by her hair. Emily hit her head on the floor, and she instantly went black. Her head instantly throbbed as everything went dark.

Everything was a blur as Emily tried to open her eyes. "I'm sure this is sacrilege… but let's face it, I'm going to Hell, anyway. What is it they preach… enjoy the life you're sinning?" She could make her out below her. Emily knew she was stretched and tied up on something. "I'm confused really, 'though shalt have no other gods before me'… does he mean God… or me, as in Julianne… I like that one, really. Makes me feel special. But I guess if he said God, then he'd just be talking in the third person, and we all know how weird that is."

Emily shook, trying to gain some composure, she could feel the sting of the wounds on her face, and she wondered how long she'd been out. Her head ached from the thump on the floor, and her stomach growled with hunger.

"'Thou shalt not take the name of the lord thy God in vain'. Well, God damn it, that sucks." Emily could see clearly enough now. She could make out her smile. "'Thou shalt not commit adultery'. Well, see, I enjoy sex too much. I don't really care if he is married or not as long as he has a nice big… wallet." Emily closed her eyes. She could hear the woman giggle. "'Thou shalt not kill'. Sheesh, these people were no fun whatsoever." Emily let her head fall back, and she realized where she was. She turned her head from side to side and knew Julianne had hung her from a cross. She watched the woman close her book and toss it back behind her. "There is one of them I like. 'Thou shall honor thy father'."

"What do you want from me?" Emily questioned.

"I personally would love nothing more than to disembowel you where you hang… that cute boyfriend of yours will come and find you. He'll be so desperate and broken-hearted I can come to his side, pretend I am just as heartbroken over the loss of a friend. And do things to him that he has only thought about in the back of his mind." Emily struggled against her bonds, and the other woman's giggle turned into a laugh. "Or maybe I'll turn his daughter into a wolf. She would be a prime candidate to be a new member of the pack."

Emily continued to struggle.

"Ah, poor puppy, I hit a nerve, did I, with your little officer?" she questioned.

"It doesn't have to be this way," Emily replied. "None of it…"

"But it does," she replied.

Emily pulled again, she could feel her wrist slip, and the bonds were not as tight as she initially thought.

Emily jerked her wrist free and quickly cut the rope with her transformed fingernails. She dropped to the floor, but the other woman only smiled wide-eyed at her. "I was wondering if you were ever going to break free." Julianne leaped. Emily turned, trying to move away, but felt the hit and was instantly knocked to the floor. She felt the woman linger over her. "I expected more of a fight." Emily turned, swinging her claws up at her attacker and connecting with her stomach. Julianne backed away, holding at her wound but continued to smile. "Here we go." She exposed the wound, and Emily could see it was only superficial. The woman showed her enlarged canines as she soared.

Emily screamed, feeling the other woman's teeth latch on. She felt her rip away, pulling at her shoulder. Emily lashed out again, claws digging into the other woman's side and chest and then collar bone with the third slash. Emily felt a claw dig into her stomach; she latched onto the other woman's arm tarring flesh to the bone. Julianne screamed. Julianne jumped off her, and Emily was quick to her feet and on top of her. Emily rolled off her, and they both were again back to their feet. Emily could see the amount of blood the other woman was losing, and it made her smile.

"I'm not as weak and helpless as you thought I was," Emily growled.

Julianne snarled, showing her enlarged canines.

"Your father didn't kill that man, did he?" Emily questioned. "You did."

"He has always tried to protect me… ever since."

"Since your mother turned you."

Julianne eyed her. The woman was hurt. It only added to her anger, and she was prepared to leap again.

"Julianne." Chamberlain's baritone voice rang through the structure. "Your father told you to leave town."

Julianna turned her back to Emily to face the approaching man. It would be so easy for her to strike, but she didn't want to kill again.

"Your father is trying to protect you from yourself. You need to learn control," Chamberlain said.

"Screw you all." Emily could hear the woman as she began to cry, and for a moment, Emily almost felt sorry for her.

"Come with me, child," he said.

Julianne growled.

"Don't do this," he said. "You'll be exiled from the pack; your father will be as well if you don't do as we ask."

"She said there were others, Alma, Morgan. They are all in danger," Emily said.

"The others are as safe as you are now," Chamberlain said.

"Who the fuck are you?" The three turned to see Kaylan Patrick with his gun raised at them, trained, specifically on Emily.

"You know who I am," Emily replied.

"Do I?" he questioned. She could hear his heart racing even from across the room.

"You only have to let me go, Kaylan," Emily replied. She kept her arms raised.

"I reported the bodies. It wasn't ten minutes after the news went out on the wire that bodies had been discovered, mauled by an animal, that my phone rang…" Kaylan said, his hand shaking. "Detective Rodney Hastings…"

Emily sighed. She looked to her left away. "He had some interesting questions… about whether there was a woman, new to our town, possibly with red hair, short or long… 5'7, thin body… he described you to a T, Sara… and then…" He fidgeted until he finally pulled the piece of paper from his back pocket, and he held it out beside his gun. Emily could see a picture of herself before the attack. "This is you… Emily Meyer."

"No," she replied.

"I'm not fucking blind. This is you," he replied.

"It was." She bit her lip, closing her eyes.

"What do you mean it was?" he asked in a confused tone. "The sheriff somehow, he fell for your ruse. But this is you."

"That was me before the attack," she replied, keeping her eyes closed.

"Being attacked doesn't change the type of person you are, the things Hastings said… accused you of… accused you of murdering his partner and countless other people. Being attacked by some animal doesn't make you an animal."

"Yes." She opened her eyes, and gone were her green eyes. She stared at Kaylan intently. "Yes, it does change you." His hand dropped in horror as he took two steps backward; tripping over his feet, he fell to the ground.

"What the fuck are you…?"

"I'm a monster," Emily replied. She took two steps forward, and Kaylan again raised his gun. "You can do it… I'm not sure it'll stop me if I really want to kill you." She approached him slowly after speaking. She leaned down as she shut her eyes. "I don't want to kill you…" She opened her eyes; the color was her normal green again. "Hastings partner… yes… I killed her. She abducted me, tied me to a chair, and I had no control then. And I killed her, all those others… the two responsible for what I am now, yes… I killed the one who turned me into this monster, but the others Hastings thinks I killed, I did not. Those men. Your friends. I did that as well. Your sheriff, he knows about us," Emily said. "Maybe you should go have this talk with him."

Kaylan looked confused, even taking several steps backward before disappearing out the door.

Emily woke. She rose as Meara was finishing the bandage on her shoulder.

"How did I get here?"

"I came and got you, three days ago," Meara replied. "I got a call from the Chamberlain. He told me where I could find you and said you'd needed some help."

"Thank you," Emily replied.

"You want to talk about it?" Meara added another stretch of tape to the wound on Emily's side. "Looks like you had quite the fight. I had to cut your clothes off you… there was… was quite a lot of blood. So much so I started to take you to the hospital…in fact if you didn't wake up today, I was going to have to come up with all kinds of convincing lies."

"Why didn't you?" Emily questioned. She hadn't even realized she was naked.

"And said what, my friend here, she's a werewolf… the wounds she has… they came from another… werewolf, and yes, please, I'll be fitted for a straitjacket now. Do they come in pink with little flowers and peace signs all over them?"

Emily smirked. "I don't think you would have had to say quite that much."

"My life has become so much more interesting since I took you in, stray cat." Meara smirked, thinking back to the first night in the alley when she was feeding all the stray cats behind Rosie's.

"I'm sorry," Emily replied, watching her patch the last wound on her arm. Emily pulled the cover up.

"I didn't say it was a bad thing," Meara replied. "I always knew there was more out there…"

"I don't know how to thank you for everything, Meara," Emily laid back.

"Take me with you," Meara said.

"Huh?" Emily gave her a stunned glance.

"You're running again, aren't you? Or maybe you'll take my advice and go see your friend Ashley and your parents…I want to go with you," Meara replied.

"Why would you?"

"Why would I want to?" Meara laughed. She washed her hands off in the kitchen sink. "I love my father, but he and I both know me staying around is only temporary. I was... I was fooling myself with the yoga shop, I know that. No one in this small town is going to do that..." Meara approached, taking a seat next to her. "Besides, you need someone to patch you up."

Emily smiled. "I am leaving... I just don't know where I'm going. And I need to say goodbye to your father, I owe him that much."

Chapter Twenty

Emily woke to the sound of someone knocking on the door. "Hello?" she called out, pulling herself up and wiping her hair from her face. She crossed into the living room; Meara's door was closed. It had been three days since she woke up, her injuries were healing but she was still feeling rough.

She opened the front door and smiled when she saw Don. "Hey, stranger." She tried to remember when was the last time she saw him "You haven't been answering your phone, haven't been to work in a week and Meara says you've had a very bad stomach bug."

"Sorry," she replied with a smile. He approached, she leaned up and gave him a kiss, and she felt her heart beat a touch faster when he smiled. *How was she going to say goodbye?* It was going to be tougher than she thought.

"No reason to be sorry… but you can make it up to me," Don replied, his eyes looking off to one side and then back to Emily.

"How?" she replied. She couldn't stop smiling.

"Go camping with me." He didn't form it as a question.

"Camping?" Emily looked at him, confused.

"Yes, camping," he said with a smile. "I promise not to bite." Emily glared and then smiled at him. "Okay, maybe a little," he replied. "So, are you in?"

"Where are we going?" she questioned, and Don replied with a big smile.

"You will need your hiking shoes." Emily looked at him, curious, wondering what he was up to, but she was happy for the surprise from him.

"Okay," she replied. "Will I need anything else?"

"An open mind?" Emily's eyes grew wide, trying to figure out what he was up to. She had already decided to leave. It was what was best for everyone for her to split town. But she owed it to Don, one night away, and she could take the time to explain it all to him. Though she knew he could take care of himself, she thought it best if she went with him on the little trip.

They had driven an hour away from town. Emily never questioned any along the way. She just sat there keeping with the chatter. She found Don interesting. He was romantic, and she trusted him. She didn't trust him enough to tell him her secret, but it was more for his safety and sanity than her need to let someone in. Even if some part of her knew he was already knowledgeable about werewolves, how could she bring him that much further into the fold. She was equally surprised when they arrived at an old campsite, and he told her it was about five miles into the wilderness, but he never told her what. She kept pace with him, letting him lead, but she knew she would have no problem upping the pace, and at times she did just to see how he would react. She topped a valley, saw a structure in the distance, and turned back to look at Don. "What is that?" she questioned.

"It is a forestry fire tower. It used to be used to spot fires in the past," he replied. "Before they started using phones. And planes, hell, still used quite frequently in some territories."

"I hope you don't expect me to climb up in that thing." She could see it was way off the ground sitting on top of one of the higher peaks around.

"We will see," he replied, taking her by the hand, pulling her along.

Emily didn't realize just how far the base was off the ground until they reached the bottom. She watched as Don removed his backpack and set it on the ground at the base of the stairs. "No way in hell…." She looked from him and then back upward. "Is it safe?"

"Even though it isn't used, every year there is a safety check. So it is perfectly safe, darling," he said with his hand outreached. She was hesitating, but she reached to put her hand in his and followed him along slowly up the stairway. They were about four stories up when Emily looked down for the first time, and she felt her entire body go weak, and then his arms wrapped around her. "Don't look down," he said, and she gave him an annoyed smile.

"Of course," she replied, taking a step forward, her legs were weak, but she focused on following him up the stairs. They reached the top and watched as he pulled the keys and opened the door. He held it open for her as she walked inside. She was happy to be on the inside of enclosed walls and felt her legs' strength come back to her. A big window on each wall allowed the forestry officers to look out over the surrounding wilderness. "Oh my," she said, stepping forward.

"Amazing, isn't it?" Don said.

She felt the tower sway. His smile gave her a nervous feeling.

"Don't worry. It has held strong for 100 years."

"Beautiful," she replied.

"Yes, you are." She turned to face him, he wasn't looking out at the wilderness, but she knew he had seen it many times before. She looked up into his eyes.

"You're too sweet," she replied.

"I'm glad you picked this town," he said, leaning forward and softly kissing her on the lips. She felt his arms wrap around her, he was warm, and she could feel his heartbeat between them. It made her think of Colin, and it made her frown.

"I'm glad I did as well." She turned and reached up, kissing him again. "I'm glad I met you." Don ran his hand through her hair, letting it rest on the back of her neck pulling her in for another kiss. She could feel his other hand on her hip, pulling her into him. She felt his free hand drift up under her shirt, and as he touched her skin, she gasped. His hands were so cold. But she didn't care. The gasp wasn't from the coolness, but his touch sent shivers up her body. She let her hands drift as she grabbed his shirt, pulling it up over his head. It was then she paused, looking around. She walked over to sit on the old bed, it wasn't comfortable, but she didn't really care. Nor was there much room on it for more than one person, and it only made her smile as she watched him approach, undoing his pants in the process. She smiled, pulling her own shirt off and tossing it to the floor.

Don stood silent.

"I had a small accident while running. Meara patched me up," Emily said.

"You're okay, right?" he questioned.

"More than just all right." She motioned for him to approach. "I bet you bring all the girls up here," she replied with a sly smile.

"Honestly…" he replied.

"No," she replied and could see it on his face this was not the first time, "Lie to me this time." She laughed as she ran her hand down his face. He was so different from Colin; she thought he was more than just serious about her. She could see it in his eyes, he was falling for her, and she sighed when the look hit her the most. She knew now more than ever that she had to leave.

"Don't…" She smirked, and he did the same. His lips quivered. She knew what he was about to say. "You barely know me."

"It is foolish, I know," he replied.

"It is foolish." She walked, looking out the window. She smiled; the view was more than just beautiful it was breathtaking. She heard him approach, slowly walking up behind her. He ran his hands up and down her arms, and she could hear his heavy breath. "You don't know me…"

"I know enough," he replied. She knew as he leaned forward when she felt his lips on the side of her neck.

"You don't," she replied. She felt tears. She didn't want to cry, but she knew she could not say the words if he did. And the last thing she wanted to do was hurt him.

"Then tell me," he replied.

"I just want you to hold me." He wrapped his arms around her, pulling her back into him. She raised her hands, placing them on his arms. She could see his reflection in the window, and she smiled. She knew she could love him in another life, but at this point, it was not the best thing for her or him.

They had traveled back down to the ground. Don had built a fire and set up a tent with sleeping bags and everything. He had packed them a dinner picnic, and a bottle of wine, and she had never even realized he was carrying so much more than her when they traveled in from the truck. "Tell me about you, Emily…"

"What do you mean?" Emily questioned. She knew where this was going, she knew exactly what he had in mind, and she just wondered if she was strong enough to tell him no. Even if it was not what she wanted.

"I mean you, I know about your friend… the attack, but I feel I don't really know that much more about you than that. It doesn't identify your life," Don said.

Emily smirked. *It does now.*

"You want my life story up to the accident." Emily smiled. "Really not a lot to tell."

"Everyone has a story," Don replied. "I told you mine once before."

Emily remembered. "I was born to loving parents, a grandmother who I remember fondly from my youth even though she passed away when I was ten. She always made the joke I was a runner because I would always go from my parents' house to hers, which at the time was about a mile apart on a one-lane dirt road. A holler in the middle of nowhere, Kentucky… After my grandmother died…" Emily paused. None of it was a lie, and she realized she was telling him the truth.

"Go on," he replied with a smile, and immediately, she could see it in his eyes. He knew what she was saying was real.

"My grandmother died, and my father took a job in West Virginia, so he uprooted us and moved us. Same type of small-town atmosphere, country hospitality of sorts if you weren't different. From there, I took my grandmother's words to heart: I ran. Every day. I joined the track teams, and anytime I could spend time on the track, I did so. When I graduated from high school, I went to West Virginia University, where I spent three years studying prelaw, then Marshal University as I tried to get a degree in law… At the time of the attack, I had taken a break from school but was working as a clerk at a law firm."

"Are your parents still living?" he questioned.

"They are," she replied, looking away from the fire.

"But they don't know where you are, do they?" he asked. Emily didn't answer and after a moment he came with a different question. "What was your grandmother's name?"

"Abby… it was short for Abigail." Emily smiled. "She used to make these wonderful gingerbread muffins that were to die for."

"Anyone special back home?"

"Ashley." Emily almost blushed. "I was a jock… she was a punk rock girl who spent some time behind the gym smoking…" Emily's eyes grew wide as she looked up at him.

"Almost everyone has tried marijuana, even me, Emily," he said with a smile.

"You should see her… she's half Cherokee and white. She dresses daily as if she is going to a rock show. Streaks of multiple colors in her hair and takes shit from no one…."

Don stood as he walked around, sitting behind Emily, letting her lean back into him. "Your smile is bright when you talk about her. You should call them… let them at least know you're okay."

"They know," she lied.

"You're lying." He pulled her tighter against him. "I can feel your heart racing as you think about them. Your pulse speeds…" She pulled her hand out of his grasp. "Everyone has their secrets, Emily."

She sat up, pulling away from him. "This is starting to feel like an interrogation."

"Aren't most dates?" Don replied.

"Yeah, but most dates aren't with enforcement officers who wanted to be a cop at one time." Emily shifted to look at him, glaring into his eyes. She stood circling back to the opposite end of the fire. "Ask me what you want to ask, you have something on your mind, and you brought me way out here. Cornering me. And I don't think this was about sex." Emily knew she wasn't cornered… the wolf wasn't cornered; she could find her way out even in the cloudy night.

"Liam Bell, you've been seeing him too. And Kaylan Patrick, if the gossip around town is to be believed." Emily could see the disappointment on his face.

"No," Emily replied, thinking about the run she took with Liam.

"The first lie you've told me." Don pulled away.

"Yes…" she stuttered, and her heart started to race. "It's complicated."

The howl of a wolf broke her attention as she turned to look out in the darkness. She knew it was not one of hers. It was a normal wolf. She could smell it on the cold night air, a few of them lingering out in the darkness, but they were far away and not coming closer. "I went for a run with him." She turned back just as Don stood. "It wasn't a date, and there is nothing there between us."

"And Kaylan?" he questioned as he placed his hand on his hips.

"We… worked out." Emily frowned, realizing how it sounded, and she could see the smirk take over his face. "I'm sorry, I promise I didn't have sex… they weren't…"

"You don't owe me an apology," Don replied. Wolves again howled off in the distance, but this sounded different from the previous howls. She watched as Don tossed a few more chopped logs onto the fire. He walked around, turning up the lantern and checking the oil level. "They won't come near the light."

"Who told you I was seeing them?"

"The talk of the town," he replied. "The four of us, it seems."

Emily frowned. "Liam is…" Emily ran her hand through her hair and was looking for something to say.

"Slimy?" Don smiled, and she broke her frown and smiled as well.

"He is sketchy, something off about him and how he acts," she replied. "And Kaylan is… I think worse in his own way."

"Then why did you go for a run with him? Or work out with Kaylan?"

"He had me trapped. The night Meara and I went to his place, I didn't want to go, and the day I went for a run, it was coincidence… or…"

"Or he was stalking you," Don replied. She could see his frown.

"Maybe, I don't know. It was my first time on that trail. It really could have just been chance that I ran into him." Emily watched him approach.

"I am sorry I questioned you," he said, and she smiled. Her heart still raced; she was lying to him. It may have just been a coincidence he was there then. But what they did together that evening, she regretted it even now.

"I should have told you I saw him…" She paused.

"We should get some sleep," Don said. "A long walk back."

"You knew, and you waited. Waited until after we came all the way out here and almost had sex." Emily was disappointed. She didn't know Don as well as she thought she did. Howls again broke her from her gaze on the man, normal wolves bellowing off in the distance.

It was early morning when Emily woke, still dark, and there was fresh snow on the ground when Emily pulled herself free and climbed from the tent. Don was still sleeping. She walked, looked up at the tower, and took a deep breath. She could still smell the wolves in the air, they had gotten closer to them in the night, and it made her heart race. She could smell the blood and flesh on their tongues, and it sent a shiver up her back. It was human blood she smelled. She could see her own breath as she moved forward; she stopped looking back at the closed tent before she slipped off into the wilderness. She could smell it, the strong smell of death and decay. She took step after step moving forward. She had relied so much on her sense of smell she never saw or heard it until it started growling. She twisted, looking to her right up an embankment as a large two-hundred-pound wolf snarled and growled at her. Saliva and blood leaked from its mouth as it took a step back from her.

Emily growled. She felt her canines grow as she did so. "Go away," she muttered. She watched the wolf back away.

It was then she saw the others, at least three other wolves, all with their focus on her. She heard the click of a safety go off, and she twisted, seeing Don with his weapon drawn and pointing in the direction of the wolves. "Don't," she said softly. Don looked to her and then to the big black alpha. She thought about the painting of the big black wolf in Liam Bell's office, blood dripping from its lips as it trailed behind a redhead. She turned, looking around and around. The entire thing sent a chill down her back.

"I'm not going to shoot," he replied. She saw three others. They circled them, but none of them approached, and she could feel their eyes on her. All of them were watching her.

"There is something wrong. Do you smell that?" she questioned. She was sure he didn't, looking back at Don as he raised his head in the air to take in a scent.

He just shook his head. "I smell wilderness… some musk or something… it's the wolves. They're soaked from the snow."

Emily knew that wasn't it. She walked forward; it was the only direction she could go without being toward a wolf they could see and the way they came.

"Where are you going?" Don questioned. She could hear his breath quicken. Emily rushed forward, still up the small hill and down the valley. She could hear Don behind her and the wolves off to her left and right, keeping pace. The smell grew now, so much so that it took her breath away. "Stop," she heard Don, and she knew he smelled it now.

"Something's…dead." Emily stopped. She looked back just as Don passed by her; he stopped a few steps away, looking around for the wolves. "Stay close." Emily walked on, but she knew now what he was going to find, a boneyard.

They topped the next hill, and as they did, a couple of wolves scattered into the unknown. "Oh my god," she heard Don say, and the sight took Emily's breath away. She looked at Don, he was ghostly white as he looked back at her and dug into his pocket, pulling out his phone, but she could tell immediately he had no service this far out into the wilderness. "Stay here," Don said, looking back at her.

Emily took a long deep breath. She didn't have to get closer. She could smell them, all of them. There were at least twelve bodies there. Some fresh, others had been here for weeks. "I can't disturb the grounds… these people have been torn apart by the wolves." Emily frowned, knowing there was more truth in his words than he'd know. "We need to go back to camp, pack up and go home. I'll take you to your truck and go report it."

Chapter Twenty-One

The smell of other werewolves took over her before they returned to the camp, at least three or even five. Julianne was one of them. She had tracked her all the way out here despite her father wanting her to leave town. "Don…" Emily paused, turning to look back at him. "I'm sorry I didn't tell you about Liam."

"I'm sorry I should have asked before we…" Don replied, taking a long deep breath. "I was an ass. We weren't exclusive… still aren't, I have nothing to be mad about, and I'm sorry."

Emily stepped in closer. She thought about running. It was still maybe an hour before daybreak. She could lead the other werewolves away from Don. She couldn't let them kill him like they did Colin. She hesitated; these were not the wolves who killed Colin. But that didn't change the fact that this would be just as much her fault if something did happen to him. And Meara would never forgive her. Emily stepped up, leaning in and slowly kissing him on the lips. "I'm sorry."

Don gave her a confused look.

Emily could hear them circling, and smell at least four distinguishable scents, two of them were in full transformation. "I'm sorry I never told you the whole story."

Emily walked past him back into the camp sight. She caught another scent now, Meara. They had dragged her all the way out here as well. Emily panicked as she rushed forward.

"The guest of honor has arrived." The bald pack member, slender built with a serpent posture, held Meara by her throat on the other side of the fire. He smiled. It was Olsen, and she now had his scent. It was very distinctive. Decay seemed to exude from him. This was his killing grounds.

"I'm sorry," Meara muttered.

"Ah, she thinks this is her fault," the man said.

"What the hell?" Don rushed forward toward his daughter. He didn't even see Julianne. She knocked him to the ground, placing her knee into his back.

"Don't do this," Emily said, looking at them. It had started to snow harder now. "Let them go. We'll settle this just you and I."

She watched the two share a glance before Julianne stood, letting Don up, and the slender man let Meara go, who quickly went to help her dad up. The two of them got behind Emily. "We've never formally met," the man said with a wicked smile. "I'm Olsen, not that you're going to be alive long enough to need it. You've messed with the dynamics of the pack, Ms. Meyer."

"I know who you are," Emily hissed.

"What is this?" Don questioned.

Emily turned, standing in the driving snow as she unbuttoned her pants, looking at Don and Meara. "You need to run…" She pushed her pants down her legs, kicking her shoes off, and she could feel the change coming on. She dropped to her knees in the snow; she felt his hands on her.

She looked up to see Meara leaning over the top of her and Don at her side. "Run," she growled. "Don't look back…" She sat up on her knees. Julianne was well into her change. Emily undid her bra. "Run!" she screamed out again she fell forward onto her hands amid the change.

Emily opened her eyes and twirled, thinking she would see Julianne, but she was nowhere to be seen. Emily howled in frustration. Olsen's eyes transformed and loomed over her looking with an eager smile. Emily knew this was it. Even if she beat Julianne, the other wolves would kill her. The only thing she could hope for was to buy her friends enough time to get away. Emily rushed forward, getting a good grasp of the other woman's scent, and slowly, she followed into the wilderness. Emily went away from where she was sitting, away from the others, but it was not far out of sight before Julianne had begun to circle around, heading in the direction of the people Emily wanted to protect. Emily picked up her pace, following Julianne's scent. Faster and faster, and then she stopped having moved a couple hundred feet from where she circled back. Emily held her head high and listened; she could hear Meara and Don as they moved frantically away from them. Emily slowly moved in their direction. She could hear three others at her back but could not place Julianne. Emily would run a few feet and slow to see if she could hear Julianne, but she was nowhere to be seen, even though her scent went in the same direction. Emily broke into a run until she was certain she was ahead of her friends, and she went into the direction they were traveling. She could see them rush forward, and knew they hadn't seen her. It was then she saw Julianne. Emily had passed her somehow as she broke into the path behind Don and Meara growling, and they knew it too.

Emily stepped in, snarling. She could see the horror on their face as they realized they were trapped between the two. Don raised his weapon quickly, pointing it at both before he settled on the lighter-colored werewolf, Julianne. He could tell the difference. Emily walked forward, and Meara was quick to move out of her way as their eyes met. Emily tried to fight it, but she snarled at Meara before she turned her attention back to Julianne. Emily approached the larger wolf. Julianne was no Madison; Madison would have made two of even Devon, but Emily wasn't as old or seasoned as Julianne. She snarled, walking past Don and keeping her eyes on Julianne. She got firmly between them, looking back at Don, and he didn't hesitate as he went and grabbed his daughter, taking back off through the wilderness away from them.

Julianne stepped forward as if she was going to go around Emily, but Emily stepped blocking the other wolves direct path. Julianne growled, and it almost sounded like a laugh to Emily as she moved in the opposite direction. Julianne acted as if he was going to try a circle her again, but again, Emily moved into her path, growling. Julianne took two quick steps backward and leaped over Emily. Emily circled into a sprint. She may not have been stronger than Julianne or as old, but she knew she was faster. Emily caught her not long after their standoff, leaping onto her back and clamping down on the back of her neck and twisting Julianne over. Both flipped on the ground, but Emily was immediately back on her feet. She watched Julianne stand, shaking off the attack.

Emily leaped knocking Julianne to her back with force, Julianne's jaws bit into Emily's shoulder and she howled out in pain. Emily glared up at Julianne, seeing her blood-soaked jowls. Emily pushed until she forced Julianne off her. Emily circled away and ran. She made sure Julianne was behind her. Emily ran as fast as she could until she stumbled, rolling forward over and over, coming to a finish on her stomach. Emily ached. Every muscle in her body was sore, and the new wound on her shoulder hurt. Even the wound on her face hurt. She twisted onto her back, knowing any moment Julianne was going to be there on top of her. She took a long deep breath, trying to gather her energy, but Julianne did not come. She sat up and growled, raising her head into the air, trying to get a bearing on where the others were. She snarled as she got to her feet, slowly, began to move back in the direction she had come, careful, watching any movement in the forest around her. She did not think she could handle another attack on her arm.

Emily moved at a steady pace until she had come back to where she had landed on Julianne. She could see her tracks leading back in the direction of the others again, Julianne was relentless, and Emily quickly broke into a sprint to catch up. It wasn't long before she came upon them. Meara was on the ground, she could see no visible wounds on her friend, but she seemed unconscious. Don sat holding his arm, there was blood, and Emily felt her heart stop. Had he been bit?

"It's simple." She saw Olson slither from the wilderness in his human form. "Change back," he growled. He stepped up behind Don putting his hand at his throat. She felt her heart stop thinking of Lauren and Colin. How could she find herself in such a similar position just a few months later? "Change back, or I'll kill your boyfriend."

Emily growled, taking a step forward, but she could see the tension in the man's arm grow. His fingernails grew longer and sharper at Don's throat. She watched Don shake his head no. "Do it!" Olsen hissed.

Emily lowered her head exposing her neck to one side. Emily looked at Meara, who lay just a few feet away. This time it was going to be different. "I haven't touched him… he won't turn." Emily looked back to Olson and then to the wound on Don's arm as she dropped to her knees. Emily was exhausted. She took a long deep breath using her wounded arm to steady herself. Every muscle in her body made a sound, loud popping as it shifted back into place. She howled as the last bit of the wolf left her, and she threw up instantly, rolling over, nude on the rough cold ground. She coughed as she tried to catch her breath. She twisted, watching the man step back away from Don.

"I made a promise, I will do no harm to him or his daughter… you just have to do one simple thing."

She rolled over, pushing herself up off the ground and into a standing position. She weaved struggling to stay upright on her weak legs.

"What?' she questioned, looking at Don now, who shook his head no. "What is it you want?" She approached, never stopping her movement until she was beside Don.

"Call it good faith that I let you get this close, to protect your cattle…"

"You bitch." Julianne stepped into the clearing, fully transformed back into her human form. She was bleeding from several wounds. Emily could smell the other wolves, so close now they could attack in any second.

Julianne leaped with her clawed hand and struck across Emily's upper chest. If she had not moved when she did, she would have slashed right through her throat. She could smell her blood as she whirled away, trying to put some space between them. It was then she felt Julianne's claws cut through her side, the same side Devon had bitten into, and it brought back memories of her initial attack. Emily twisted at the cut and screamed. She attacked out wildly, trying to get the other woman off her.

Julianne tried to bite her, but she found there was just enough space between their bodies; Emily lifted her knees, pushing up against Julianne and away from her just in time to hear her teeth chomp at the air.

Emily flipped Julianne onto her back, she felt the air go from Julianne as they landed, and Emily pushed her weight around until she had Julianne's arms held above her head motionless. She turned to look at Don. He had helped Meara from the ground, and both were looking at Emily.

Emily gave Julianne one last glance before she fell over onto her back and looked up at the stars, it was beginning to break daylight on the horizon. She smiled. The shadows of Don and Meara eclipsed her as she shut her eyes. She felt him pull her, dragging her to her feet, and she opened her eyes to see Meara.

"It's bad," she heard Don say but could not see him as she weaved forward into Meara's arms.

She took a long deep breath, and her eyes opened. She twisted, still needing them to hold her up in an upright position. She saw the figures emerge from the shadows, werewolves walking toward them. Emily recognized Harrison and Morgan in front of the group.

Emily growled, falling forward out of Don's grip. She pushed herself up onto her knees, looking at them as they moved toward them in the fog. Then she saw the dark wolf emerge from the others and disappear. It was not long before Alma stood there naked in the morning light over her. There was another scent there as a large dark wolf stepped out of the wilderness, seeming to give Alma a nod of approval. Liam.

Epilogue

Ten days had passed since the events in the woods. With dark sunglasses covering her eyes, Emily sat staring out the window. Oakridge almost seemed peaceful. Almost like a home now. She took a deep breath.

"Give him time," Alma said, wrapping her arms around her. "He has been introduced to a new world. You can't expect him to be okay only a few days later."

"But he already knew about us…" She looked at the woman before returning to look outside.

"It's not easy, he went from just knowing to being fully a part of the world, and you have to give him time," Alma said. "Everything will be all right."

"How do you know that?" Emily questioned.

"You are now a member of the pack," Alma said with a smile. Her long black fingernails clicked on the table, drawing Emily's attention. It was then she saw the large oval gem on her ring finger.

"You're engaged," Emily said in excitement.

"Marion's a good man," Alma said.

"But do you love him?" Emily questioned.

There was a sense of hesitation in Alma's expression. "Yes, I believe I do love him. And I want you to come to the wedding…"

Emily opened her mouth to speak.

"I will not take no for an answer." She kissed Emily on the cheek before standing up. She had a large smile on her face as she left the diner.

Emily made sure everyone was gone before she turned on the computer and instantly sent the video message. It was only a moment before Ashley answered, and she couldn't contain her smile. "Hey, love."

"Hey," Ashley replied. A moment after, her mom appeared. It looked like she had aged ten years in just a few short months.

"Emily." She put a hand over her mouth. Hearing her mom's voice made her want to burst into tears. "Are you okay?"

"I'm…" Emily paused. "I'm fine, Mommy." She didn't know what to say. She had no believable excuse to tell her mom. Not looking her in the eyes, she couldn't lie to her.

"Where are you?" her mom questioned.

"I'm sorry," Emily replied.

"Where are you?" she repeated her question.

"I'm safe," Emily said.

"The wolf, they put it down," Emily recalled the story Ashley told her about the dead wolf. "There were so many wild stories. Every hunter around claimed they'd seen a black panther to Bigfoot, but it was a wolf. It traveled so far from its home. You can come home."

"I want to," Emily answered, forcing a smile. She could feel the tears just below the surface, it wouldn't be much, and she'd be bawling her eyes out.

"Then come home." She could see Ashley, remaining silent, in tears standing behind her mom.

"I promise I will." Emily forced a smile.

Her mom smiled.

"I need to go, Mom. I will call soon." Emily didn't want to cry. She couldn't fight back the tears any longer.

"Promise me," her mom replied.

"I promise." Emily knew why. She'd never broken a promise she'd made to her mother.

"I love you," her mom said.

"I love you both." She watched as Ashley blew her a kiss just before she shut her laptop.

Emily sat back, taking a deep breath, shutting her eyes, and trying to control her emotions. She didn't want to cry.

"Miss Emily Meyer."

Emily opened her eyes. She didn't expect to see Detective Rodney Hastings again. She could smell the liquor on his breath and the smell of gun oil from the freshly cleaned gun he no doubt had pointed at her under the table. "We have a lot to talk about." There was another scent more powerful than all the others. She could smell the wolf that Hastings had become.

About the Author

Steven Paul Watson is many things: a writer, artist, amateur photographer, and avid outdoorsman as well as an all-around geek. His love of writing includes soul-chilling science fiction, fantasy, all things supernatural/horror, and a passion for steampunk/alternate reality.

In his free time spends a lot of time out in nature hiking the hills near his home. There is no better way to stroke one's imagination than being outdoors in the wilderness having real adventures that feed the ones he puts on a page. Steven is also an avid crafter and artist making a lot of jewelry and woodcrafts. Loves dogs and spending time with his family.